TALES FROM CABIN 23

NIGHT OF THE LIVING HEAD

TALES FROM CABIN 23

NIGHT OF THE LIVING HEAD

HANNA ALKAF

SERIES CREATED BY

JUSTINA IRELAND & HANNA ALKAF

Balzer + Bray

An Imprint of HarperCollins*Publishers*

ALSO BY HANNA ALKAF

The Girl and the Ghost

Hamra and the Jungle of Memories

For Malik and Maryam, and for the kids who always wanted to see themselves face the darkness . . . and win.

Because you can win. You can make it through.

I believe in you.

AT CAMP APPLE HILL FARM THERE IS A STORY:

For a few campers a mysterious fog will appear, summoning them to a witch's cabin where they must endure a terrifying tale . . . or else! Why the cabin appears is not truly known, although many theories abound. The cabin does not exist on any map, and while many campers have gone looking for this mysterious cabin, few have found it, but those who do tell of a terror that defies explanation.

ARE YOU BRAVE ENOUGH TO VISIT CABIN 23?

PROLOGUE

The sliver of moon that hung in the sky wouldn't have been much help in illuminating Melur's path anyway, but the way it kept playing peekaboo behind the clouds made it seem like it was making her journey harder on *purpose*.

"Aah!"

Someone—something?—tugged at her hijab, stopping Melur in her tracks. She whirled around, fists up, heart pounding. "Who's there?" she called. "Who did that? Who—" The words died on her lips as she found herself yelling in the face of . . . a tree branch.

"Oh." She tugged her crooked hijab back into place. "That's all right then," she told the tree, as if it could understand her.

It was her own fault, really. After all, she was the one who'd convinced her mother this two-week summer camp experience would be good for her, even though her mother had sighed over the cost, and worried over how far away it was. "All the way in America!" Ibu had said, biting her lip. "You had to find the one camp as far away from Malaysia as possible, is it?" Melur had persuaded her they could combine it with a visit to her cousin in New York, promised to check in every day as long as it was within the hours mandated by the rules, and agreed to add everything on Ibu's long list of must-haves for keeping her safe—from Tiger Balm to Mopiko to a copy of the Qur'an—to her suitcase until Ibu had eventually caved in.

But the Camp Apple Hill Farm experience wasn't exactly what Melur had imagined it would be, as far away as it was from home—even if she could never admit that to her mother. She'd planned for bugs and outdoor adventures and rustic wooden cabins. She just hadn't thought about living with all these strange girls, or how all the food tasted bland and gray, or how the air even *smelled* different here, or how leaving a place where you were certain you belonged could sometimes feel like waking up with a hole in your chest.

And Melur had definitely never imagined her camp experience to include walking into the deep dark of the woods in the middle of the night.

She'd been careful, before she took a single step beyond the tree line. She'd given salaams, asked permission to enter. But you could never be sure, after all, if Western ghosts followed Malaysian rules.

"You could just choose truth," Lou had whispered as they huddled together with their three other roommates on the floor of Cabin 17. Their flashlight slashed weak white beams over their faces, making everyone look like ghosts. "You don't have to take the dare." Melur had known Lou was the nicest of them all since day one, when they'd been the one to invite her to walk together to the welcome jamboree and then spent the night hassling the counselors until someone finally produced a bag of halal marshmallows for the Muslim campers.

But not everyone was like Lou. And not everyone understood what kinds of secrets Melur was keeping.

Melur set her jaw and crossed her arms. What had Ibu always told her? "Don't go telling people our business." She was a person who kept her truths to herself. She wasn't about to start sharing them with a bunch of kids she barely knew and would probably never see again, even if she wanted desperately to fit in with them at the same time. "Dare," she said, and her voice echoed through the dark cabin.

Dara—pretty, perfect, popular Dara—had tossed her dark curls. "Then I dare you to walk out into the woods and *find the witch*."

Everyone gasped. "Not the witch!" Lou squealed, then quickly clapped their hand over their mouth when Dara glared at them.

"Quiet! We'll get caught!"

"Sorry," Lou mumbled. "Sorry, Dara. It's just that . . . I mean . . . we've all heard the story, right? About that girl last year who went out to Cabin twenty-three?"

The others nodded solemnly. "I didn't," Melur said. "What happened to her?"

Lou leaned forward, their eyes wide. "She *never. Came. Back. Out.*"

Melur frowned. "If she never came back out, how do you know the story?"

"Never mind that!" Dara snapped. "*Everyone* knows that the witch of Cabin twenty-three lures you out there, trapping you inside the cabin to tell you—"

"The scariest story you've ever heard," said Lakshmi in her thick British accent. A shiver ran down Melur's spine. There was something about the way her cabin-mates were talking and the way the light cast weird shadows on their faces that almost made her believe

4

their silly little ghost story. "What story do you think she'll tell you?"

"I don't know." Melur gulped. "Do I really have to—"

"*Yes.*" Dara's eyes gleamed in the glow of the flashlights. "Why? Are you too chicken?"

Melur grit her teeth. "Of course not," she lied. "If there's a witch out there, I'll find her. And I'll bring back a souvenir to prove it."

Lou tugged urgently at Melur's sleeve. "*Souvenir??* It's not *Disneyland*," they hissed. "It's the *witch*. Are you sure about this?"

Melur caught a glimpse of Dara's smirk and whatever fear she had was immediately squashed by the knowledge that she had to do whatever it took to wipe the smirk off Dara's face. "It'll be fine," she told Lou. "I'll be back before you know it."

And so here she was, fighting with trees in the middle of the night, muttering Ayat Kursi to herself as she walked. Behind her, she could see Cabin 17 in the distance, the girls a faint speck on its wooden deck. She gave them a tentative wave. If she squinted, she thought someone—probably Lou—waved back. But it was hard to be sure.

"All right," Melur said, stopping at last. "Now to

find the witch." She turned back to the girls for one last look. Not that she wasn't coming back. She just felt like it, that was all.

But Cabin 17 was gone.

Melur blinked. "What the—"

All around her, a fog was rising from the ground, enveloping everything in cool white, and growing thicker and thicker until it became hard to see.

Melur gulped.

"This is probably silly, right?" she asked aloud, to nobody in particular. "I'm walking into the woods to find an urban legend. A figment of everyone's imagination. That's ridiculous behavior, right? Right. I'm just going to—" She turned around, poised to start running back to the safety of her cabin as fast as she could. Who cared if Dara laughed at her and called her chicken, anyway? Chickens got an unfairly bad rap, if you asked Melur.

But the fog had other ideas. White tendrils wrapped themselves around her wrist so that she couldn't move. Melur couldn't tell if the goose bumps on her skin were from their ice-cold touch, or the fear that had lodged itself in her throat and made it hard for her to breathe. All around her there was nothing but a wall of white.

Melur was about to scream when the mist before her cleared a little—just enough to make out a path ahead of her. *Thank goodness.* She began to walk, and with each step, the fog seemed to recede a little more, until at last she found herself on the edge of a clearing awash in moonlight, every leaf and blade of grass so illuminated, it was like they were lined in silver.

Which was weird, because the moon had been barely a crescent when she started out.

Ahead of her, in the middle of the clearing, stood a cabin that she'd never seen before—at least, not on the tour of the campgrounds they'd been given on day one. It didn't, as far as she could see, look terribly different from her own, except that the porch sagged, and some shingles were missing from the moss-covered roof, and the numbers had been knocked out of place, the two lying forlornly on its side, the three leaning to the right.

"Cabin twenty-three." Melur bit her lip so hard, she tasted blood.

And then, as she watched, the lights within suddenly flicked on.

Every nerve in Melur's body was telling her this was a bad, bad idea. She turned to go, but the wall of fog blocked her way, as impenetrable as rocks.

Behind her, there was a long, loud creaking sound as the door swung open.

Slowly, she turned back around.

A figure stood in the doorway, light streaming from behind so that all she could see was a dark silhouette.

Melur felt cold sweat snaking its way down her face.

The figure moved forward, and features swam into focus. A brown-skinned woman stood before her, dark hair tied back in a low ponytail. She was dressed in the same camp T-shirt and khaki pants the rest of the counselors wore. But Melur hadn't seen her before either.

"So you're finally here," the woman told her, and her voice was low and pleasant. "Come inside. Warm yourself by the fire, and have a nice hot drink." The woman licked her lips and smiled. "Everything tastes better . . . hot."

Before Melur could say anything, she felt the fog pushing her from behind. The woman stepped smartly aside as Melur was swept in through the door and into a worn wooden chair by a crackling fire. "Thank you!" the woman said, and Melur could have sworn the fog bowed to her before it whooshed out, slamming the door behind it.

"Now then!" The woman pushed a steaming mug into Melur's hands. "Drink up."

Melur sniffed the contents suspiciously. "What . . . is it?"

The woman's smile was wide and warm. "It's not poison, silly. It's Milo."

A different kind of warmth creeped up through Melur's chest, warding off the chill of fear for just a moment. "Milo?" she whispered. Milo was the chocolate drink of her childhood; it reminded her of school sports days and rainy evenings and roti canai breakfasts at her favorite stall. Milo was home, and she hadn't quite realized until then just how much she missed belonging somewhere without even having to try.

She blinked back her tears. She wanted so badly to take a sip, wanted so badly to feel, at least for a moment, like she'd found a pocket of home in this strange, faraway place. But Melur was Malaysian, and if there was one thing Malaysian kids knew, it was to not mess with the things that were clearly supernatural.

She set the cup carefully back on the table. "No, thank you," she said politely.

"No?" the woman said. In the flickering firelight, she looked either very young or very old by turns. There was something about the way she never stopped smiling, something about the way her eyes flitted up and down Melur's whole frame, that made Melur uneasy. "Well that's . . . disappointing."

Melur couldn't help it, then. She sprang up and bolted for the door, heart pounding in her ears. If she could run fast enough, far enough . . .

The door held fast. No amount of handle-rattling or shoving would make it move. "HELP!" Melur bellowed. She banged on the shut door until her fists hurt; she yelled until her voice dried up to nothing. And all the time the woman stood, stirring the Milo in her cup with a spoon and humming tunelessly to herself.

At last Melur stopped and turned to face her captor, swallowing hard. "I know what you are," she said, her voice barely a whisper. "And I don't want your story. I want to go back."

"Do you want to go back?" The Counselor stared at her. "Or do you want to go home, Melur?"

Melur's lips trembled. Cold sweat dripped from beneath her hijab. "I never told you my name," she said.

"And yet I knew it anyway."

"What do you want from me?"

The Counselor shrugged. "I just want to tell you a story."

"Why?"

"Because, my dear." The Counselor leaned forward, her grin wide, her teeth gleaming wickedly in the firelight. "Because I'm hungry, and I can smell your fear, taste bits of it already, even—" She stuck out a long, pink tongue and licked the air, sighing with satisfaction. "And it tastes *delicious*. And I want more. More fears and more nightmares, until my belly is full and I can sleep once more."

Melur closed her eyes. "I didn't think you were real," she whispered.

"You hoped I wasn't." The Counselor laughed. "But deep down, I think you knew. You wouldn't have found the cabin otherwise." She reached out to run one cold finger along Melur's cheek, and Melur trembled beneath her touch. "Are you ready, my dear? Because I've got just the thing for you: a story of secrets and ghosts and a little girl haunted by both. I call this one *Night of the Living Head*."

Nur Alia Intan Marzuki—Alia to her friends—was born in the middle of a monsoon thunderstorm on Friday the thirteenth, and the universe never let her forget it. Her shoelaces never stayed tied, her dark, wavy hair was always working its way out of her usual ponytail, her clothes never stayed neat, her books somehow always managed to get dirty or torn, and she'd racked up more trips than an explorer, with the matching atlas of bruises across her brown skin to prove it.

Perhaps unluckiest of all, her parents had up and moved her family back to middle-of-nowhere Negeri Sembilan three months ago, where they'd lived for the first few years of Alia's life. Never mind that Alia had been perfectly happy where she was, with her old room and her friends and her school right in the heart of Kuala Lumpur. Never mind how hard she'd cried and begged and pleaded to stay when they told her. Never mind that they'd never even *asked*. And all so her father could take on a new job at the university here and her mother could go on sabbatical to write the book she'd always wanted to write on Malaysian fungi.

Fungi.

Alia didn't know which was worse: the move or that she ranked lower in importance than mold and mushrooms.

"I'm cursed," she told her parents as she stabbed at the mound of noodles on her plate. Sometimes, when her mother had too much to do, dinner came from the closest mamak restaurant, in brown paper packets with dark patches where the grease soaked through. This was one of those times. "Friday the thirteenth. It's the only explanation. Why else would all of this happen to me? How else would we have ended up back here?" She gestured vaguely toward the living room, where there were still boxes piled in the corner even though they'd already lived here for months. Most of them were full of Papa's puppets. Papa's expertise was in Nusantara culture and heritage, and the art of wayang kulit was his pet passion. He had a whole collection of the intricately carved, brightly painted leather figures used in the traditional Malay shadow theater, and every day he swore he would "get around to unpacking those," and then never did.

"If you must be superstitious, dear," Mama said, "couldn't you at least pick a Malaysian superstition instead of a Western one? We really must work on decolonizing your narratives."

"I'm only just turning twelve," Alia explained patiently. "I don't know what that means." Sometimes it was hard having such super-smart parents.

"It means you should look at things as yourself," Mama explained. "And not the way someone from another culture tells you to. Where's your sense of patriotism? We have a lot of homegrown, perfectly useful superstitions right here for you to believe in."

"Like what?"

"Like always washing your feet before bed or never stepping on a book. Or the number four, for instance!" Papa set down his fork and leaned forward, chomping thoughtfully on a mouthful of noodles. Alia sighed inwardly. Papa had his professor voice on—that meant he could go on for hours if they didn't stop him. "There is a belief that the number four is unlucky because it sounds like 'death' in most Chinese dialects, and . . ."

"How is any of that *useful*?"

Papa smiled. "Luckily, there's no four to be found anywhere in your birth date."

Alia stared at him across the dinner table. "One plus three is four," she said. "Which means I'm unlucky in *multiple cultures*."

To this, her parents just laughed.

But the thing was, Mama and Papa just didn't get it.

Ever since they moved here, the things happening to Alia didn't just feel unlucky. They felt downright creepy. She couldn't move around the house—an old thing with odd little nooks and crannies, with funny noises at night that Papa told her were "just the pipes"—without feeling that she was being watched. Or she'd be trying to get to the bathroom at school when she'd hear a sudden *whoosh* just behind her, as if something was swooping quickly past. But when she turned around, there'd be nothing there, and then she'd bump into a wall or a pole or something and bruise an elbow. Or she'd swear she saw something— someone?—moving in the shadows of the trees as she walked past. But try as she might, nothing appeared no matter how hard she looked, and then she'd trip and skin her knees. Again.

Can you be haunted by your own bad luck? Alia often wondered.

On no day was that more apparent than today. Because today was Friday the thirteenth, her birthday. And it was shaping up to be the worst one of her life so far.

For one thing, there was her black canvas school shoe, the sole of which had spent most of the day slowly unpeeling itself, so that Alia had to do a kind of shuffle-flap to get around.

For another thing, because of the shuffle-flap, she was late going down to recess when the bell rang at ten a.m. and arrived just in time to see Su Ann snag the last piece of fried chicken.

"Sorry, sorry, no more," Uncle Christopher, who managed the canteen, said apologetically, and Su Ann had smiled a smug, satisfied sort of smile.

"So sorry, Alia," she cooed. "I just beat you to it!"

"Oh," Alia said, swallowing her disappointment. "That's fine. Who needs fried chicken at this time of the morning, anyway? It'll just give you pimples or something."

Su Ann tossed her perfect ponytail. "It's a good thing I don't really get pimples," she said, before taking a bite of her chicken.

It figures, Alia thought. She'd only been here for three months, but she'd bet her entire allowance that Su Ann had never had an unlucky day in her *life*. She moved like she was always dancing to invisible music, she had perfect penmanship, and she never got less than a 90 percent on a test.

Just like when they were little.

Not that Su Ann ever gave any indication that she remembered all the days they'd spent shrieking together in an inflatable paddling pool in Alia's driveway or playing fairies beneath the trees in Su Ann's garden. These days Su Ann preferred to pretend Alia didn't exist at all, unless it was to smirk at her and say something that made her feel about two centimeters tall.

Alia might not remember much about this town, but she did remember Su Ann.

For a third thing, Alia had the feeling that she was being watched again. All day long something moved just on the edge of her sight, right at the corner of her eye, and she had the nagging idea that if she turned her head fast enough, she could catch it and figure out what it was.

And then there was the Pen Incident.

Alia had a bad habit of biting the ends of her pens as

she worked. She swore it helped her think better, even though Mama hated it ("This is plastic, Alia; you are ingesting *plastic*! That can't be good for your insides!"). It was after recess, and everyone was particularly full and sleepy. It was taking extra concentration—and extra biting—to make sure she understood exactly what Mrs. Sumathi was even saying.

"Now take out your red pens," Mrs. Sumathi said, her voice somehow extra loud in the afternoon heat. "Exchange books with the person next to you. We will go over the exercises we just completed, and you will mark them for your friend." Alia passed her book wordlessly to Charlene on her right and took her book in return. Then, chewing on the end of her pen, she began running through the sums written on the page in Charlene's neat, rounded handwriting, admiring the shapes of the numbers. Teachers always complained that Alia's own handwriting looked like chicken scratches.

And then she heard it. That familiar sound she'd come to hate.

A *whoosh* outside the window.

Oh no.

Slowly, Alia turned to her left, where the slats of the window were open to let in any stray breezes that came wafting by. The classroom was up on the first floor, and from where she sat, she could see the frangipani trees below, their boughs heavy with white blossoms.

And through them, just between the flowers, something else as well. A dark, shadowy mass. Something, Alia suddenly realized, her heart beginning to pound like a drum in her chest, that was watching her *back*.

Right then, the shadow moved. Alia bit down on her pen, hard.

The scream, when it came, almost made her jump out of her own skin.

"Really, girls," Mrs. Sumathi said, her eyes still on the whiteboard as she wrote. "No need for such drama. It's just *maths*."

"Alia!" Charlene was staring at her in horror, eyes and mouth both wide open. "Alia, what's wrong? What happened?"

"What?" Alia quickly shook herself out of her stupor and realized the entire class was staring at her. "What's going on?" And then it dawned on her that something didn't quite feel right. There was a bitterness on her tongue that hadn't been there before.

Then she looked down at her hands . . .

. . . which were covered in bright red.

Oh no.

Suddenly she forgot all about whooshes and shadows.

"Mrs. Sumathi!" Charlene shrieked. "Mrs. Sumathi! Something is terribly wrong with Alia, come and look. . . ."

Mrs. Sumathi finally glanced over, hand still hovering over the whiteboard, and promptly dropped her marker. "My god, my god," she said, hand clasped over her mouth. "What happened, child? What have you done?"

"It's just—" Alia tried to explain about the pen and the ink and the way it must have started leaking without her realizing it, but she could barely speak over the panicked shrieks of the other girls. The taste of the red liquid in her mouth was terrible. "May I go to the bathroom?" she yelled over the din.

Mrs. Sumathi strode over, ignoring her. "Let me see what's wrong—oh god, no, I cannot, there's so much blood—"

"It's not blood," Alia protested, but her words were drowned out by screams as their formidable mathematics teacher swayed slowly on her feet, rolled her eyes, and then crumpled in a heap on the floor.

There was complete silence in the classroom.

"You *killed* her," Su Ann whispered.

Their class monitor, Farah, a girl with a hijab, dark-rimmed glasses, and an unshakable calm, leaned all the way over her desk to see. "She's not dead," she reported, her voice steady and loud. "Her chest is moving, see? She must have fainted. Because of all the blood."

"It's not blood," Alia said again, only this time everyone heard her, and she shrank under their gazes. "It's . . . uh . . . it's ink," she finished lamely.

"Ink." Su Ann stared at her with narrowed eyes. "You caused all this trouble . . . over some ink."

Alia wondered for a moment what Su Ann would do if she told everyone about the time she'd gleefully pulled down her pants and gone streaking around the garden yelling "Look at my butt! Look at my butt!"

"It's not her fault!" Charlene said, and Alia shot her a grateful look. "You all *know* how Alia is!"

Okay, maybe just a little bit less grateful. "Yeah, it really wasn't my fault! I—"

"Here," Farah interrupted. "We can't leave Mrs. Sumathi like that. Come on, help me get her up on the chair. Lisa, go wet a cloth so we can wipe her face. Vidhya, get a cup of water from the canteen, will you?

And Alia . . . you better go wash up before she wakes up and freaks out again."

And so Alia spent a good half an hour standing at the sinks in the bathroom trying to scrub ink from her mouth and face and hands. *It's no wonder Mrs. Sumathi fainted*, she thought, staring at herself in the mirror. She looked as if she was covered in her own blood—or someone else's. Like some kind of hantu or vampire, a creature of nightmares.

Alia sighed. *Happy birthday to me.*

The problem with superstitions, Alia reflected as she jumped off the school bus at 1:30 p.m., was that they allowed you to believe you had some kind of control over the bad stuff that happened to you. It made sense, right? If you avoid walking under ladders, you wash your feet before bed, you replace the 4 with 3A in buildings and on houses, you stay home on Friday the thirteenth, then maybe, just maybe, you can trick the universe into being nice to you.

But you can't avoid yourself. And it was Alia herself, she decided, who was really the source of all the bad luck. *Whooshes and shadows!* she scoffed inwardly. As if the wind and sun were responsible for her own mistakes and mishaps. *Silly Alia.*

She was still thinking about this as she reached her front door, kicked off her flappy shoes, and fished for the key she wore on a long chain, hidden beneath her uniform. "I'm home," she called out as she pushed the door open.

"Alia!" Mama emerged from the kitchen, wearing her favorite apron and a strange, worried expression. From behind her wafted a hodgepodge of delicious smells: sambal and curry and lemongrass and fried things. "You're home!"

"Yes," Alia agreed. "I am."

Papa appeared from the living room, his bushy brows furrowed. "Hello, hello! You're home!"

"Y-es," Alia said again. "I . . . am."

"Did you see that, sayang? Alia's home!" Papa said, his voice sounding strangled, his smile straining at the edges.

"Yes," Mama trilled. "Yes, she's home!"

"I'm home, all right." Alia began to back away slowly. "I'm just going to . . . go up to my room and shower. . . ." Her parents often talked in ways she couldn't understand, but this was next-level weirdness, even for them.

Mama and Papa exchanged alarmed glances. "Alia, wait!" Mama called after her.

"I know, I know—don't take too long and don't forget Zohor," she shot back, bounding up the stairs two at a time and almost tripping on the third-to-last step.

"No, that's not—"

Alia wrenched open the door of her bedroom, and the rest of Mama's words were swallowed up by her own suddenly racing heartbeat thumping in her ears.

Because there was a girl, a girl who stood in front of the window, her back to Alia, nothing but a silhouette against the sunlight. A girl who was a good head and shoulders taller than Alia, with long dark hair that hung straight past her shoulders, and a baju kurung covered in pale yellow daisies, a gauzy white scarf wrapped around her neck. A girl who, when she turned, had a face in which Alia could pinpoint her own features—the bump of a nose and thick slashes of eyebrows that came from Papa, the slant to the eyes and the tiny dent in the chin that came from Mama—but older and more lived-in.

The girl had a box in her hand, wrapped in shiny pink paper.

"Happy birthday, Alia," she said.

Alia took a deep, shaky breath. "Who are you?" she asked, her voice jabbing sharply at the silence between them.

"Don't you recognize me?" The strange girl smiled a sad little smile. "I'm Ayu. I'm your sister."

The box held a pair of shoes. School shoes. Black and sensible, with Velcro straps. They were just the right size.

Alia stared at them, and then up at the girl, and then back at the shoes. "How did you know?" she asked. It seemed like a reasonable question, considering she hadn't seen her sister in years.

The girl shuffled her feet, tugging at the scarf around her neck. "Oh, Mama mentioned something. . . ." she murmured.

"Oh." This made sense. Alia clung to it like it was a life raft in the sea of Nothing-Else-Makes-Sense. Something snagged at her thoughts. "So . . . you've been talking to Mama." She didn't know why this bothered her so much.

"Yeah." The girl shuffled her feet. "And Papa."

"For how long?"

"Um." It took a minute for the girl to respond. "A couple of months now, maybe?"

"Oh," Alia said again. "A couple of months." She swallowed hard. A couple of months since they'd been talking, three since Alia and her parents had moved back to this town where they'd once been a family of four.

Her parents had known this moment was coming. And they hadn't bothered to warn her.

The silence between them grew until Alia thought she might explode from awkwardness.

"Girls!" Mama called from downstairs, and they both jumped. "Lunch is ready!"

"Coming!" the girl yelled back, as naturally as if she'd always done it. "Come on, let's go. You can shower later." And she turned and walked out of the room.

Alia drifted along behind her. She wondered briefly if this was real or if she was about to wake up covered in drool in the middle of maths again, with Mrs. Sumathi beside her wearing a grim expression. *Now please explain the work for question five, Alia. . . .*

It had been years since they'd last seen her sister. Literal, actual years. And now she thought she could just walk back into their lives without any explanation?

Talk about bad luck.

At the bottom of the stairs, Papa stood and smiled as he watched them descend. "You're home," he whispered, tears glinting in his eyes. "You're really home."

This time, Alia knew it wasn't her he was talking to.

The girl stood on her tiptoes to kiss him gently on the cheek. "Yes," she said quietly. "I really am."

Mama scooped steaming-hot rice onto everyone's plates. "Take, everyone, faster take some food," she said. Obediently, Alia put spoonfuls of food onto her own plate like she was on autopilot: prawns in fiery red sambal; a rich, thick curry full of chunks of fish and okra; her favorite spinach-and-fish-ball soup. Never mind that her stomach felt like it was twisted up into a ball of tight little knots.

The girl, she noticed, ate like a bird, pecking away at bits and pieces while telling Mama how delicious everything was. "It's been a long time since I've had food as good as this," she said. "Nobody cooks like you, Mama."

And Mama beamed so hard, it was as if her face would split in two. "Oh, you," she simpered. "It's nothing. And anyway, it's all Alia's favorites since it's her birthday today. The big one-two!" She turned the full force of her smile onto Alia, who promptly dropped a prawn onto her own lap. Red oil seeped into the gray fabric of her favorite sweatpants. Mama's smile wavered slightly at the edges as Alia scooped the prawn up and popped it into her mouth.

"What?" Alia mumbled. "It's still good."

Mama cleared her throat. "You've gotten so thin," she said, turning back to the girl and trying to ladle more food onto her plate. "Eat, eat."

"Okay, Ma, okay."

Alia watched as Mama smiled and tucked a strand of this strange girl's hair behind her ear. Something about it made her feel like someone was pinching her heart, hard. "What do I call you, anyway?" she said loudly, and her mother jerked her hand back with a start.

The girl cocked her head to one side, but slowly, as if her neck hurt. "When you were little, before . . ." Her voice trailed off. "I mean, in the old days, you called me Kak Long. Because that's what I was. Am. Your big sister." She smiled.

Alia didn't smile back. "I don't think I can call you that."

"Um."

It was pretty satisfying, watching everyone squirm in their seats.

"Well. You could call me . . . Kak Ayu?"

Alia thought about this. It wasn't as disrespectful as just using the girl's name, and it wasn't as familiar as Kak Long. She'd call complete strangers "kak," just as she would "auntie" or "uncle," just to be polite. And that's what this person was. A stranger.

"That works." She shrugged, then pretended not to notice the relief on everyone's faces.

"I can't believe you're twelve," Kak Ayu said. She fidgeted with the scarf again, fingers fluttering along the lace trim. "The last time I saw you, you must have been . . . what was it . . ."

"Six," Alia said. "I was six when you left. About to turn seven. You missed my birthday." Everyone was squirming again, but she didn't care. It was the truth, wasn't it? Why were they so set on pretending? "We do remember that she left, right?" Alia said, louder this time. "She *left* us."

"We remember," Mama said. "Of course we remember."

"Then why are we acting like we don't?"

"Because," Papa said firmly. "Because what's important isn't that she left, but that she came back."

The table was silent. Kak Ayu looked down at her hands, her plate of food still practically untouched. Her head hung low, as if it was too heavy for her neck.

Mama attempted a smile and grabbed the bowl of rice. "Who's ready for a second helping?"

She left on a Tuesday.

Alia remembered this because every Tuesday Papa came home early, and he'd take Alia to the playground, and Kak Long usually tagged along even though at sixteen—a whole nine years older than Alia—playgrounds really weren't cool anymore. But she went anyway, because Kak Long was Alia's best and most beloved playmate. She was the one person in the family who could always be relied on to make up stories for her Barbies to act out, or watch *The Little Mermaid* over and over again, or make her kaya-and-butter sandwiches anytime she asked. And Kak Long knew the playground was one of Alia's favorite places in the world. It had ladders and ropes to climb up and down, and little enclosed cubbies connected by rope bridges and cargo nets and monkey bars. There were three different slides, including one that looped round and round—that was the one Alia liked best. There were swings. There were even trampolines built right into the ground. It was a bit of a trek for Alia's little legs, but Kak Long held her hand all the way, and she never, ever complained. And when she did get tired, Kak Long gave her piggyback rides and told her bad jokes until she thought her tummy would burst from giggling so much.

Alia loved Kak Long with her whole heart, and Kak Long loved her right back.

Kak Long and Papa and Mama, though? That was another story. Alia didn't understand a word of what they were talking about when they yelled at each other, but she knew enough to hate it. She would stuff her fingers in her ears and watch Papa's face grow serious and frowny, and Mama's face grow sad, and Kak Long's face shine with angry tears, and wonder when it would all stop.

That Tuesday was when it all stopped.

Alia woke up from her afternoon nap—which she hadn't wanted to take; she wasn't a baby anymore, honestly, she was *almost seven*—to chaos. Papa was on the phone talking in his I'm-trying-my-hardest-not-to-get-angry-but-you're-making-it-difficult voice, and Mama was on the sofa crying, and Kak Long . . . Kak Long wasn't anywhere.

"Kak Long went away for a while," Mama had explained, drawing Alia close and trying to keep the hiccups out of her voice. "But she'll be back soon."

That was it, really. That was the day Alia started tripping and slipping. That was the day the bad luck came for good. Maybe she was just used to Kak Long being around, looking out for her. Maybe Kak Long took all the luck away when she left. Whatever it was, that's how Alia learned some hard lessons: to pick herself back up; to plan around and patch up the missing and lost and broken; and to ensure that her parents were never, ever hurt like that again.

So you'd think Alia could be forgiven for not quite jumping on the WELCOME HOME, AYU bandwagon. You'd think she could get a little understanding of what it was like to live in the shadow someone else left behind for almost half of your life. You'd think her super-smart parents would understand that you can't just go back to being sisters after *five whole years of nothing*.

But no. Instead, here Kak Ayu was, invading Alia's whole life. One more place at the table, one more person in line for the bathroom, one more device hogging the Wi-Fi, one more portion at meals. And worst of all: one more person in her room.

"What do you mean we have to share?" Alia stared at Papa, open-mouthed. "You cannot be serious. This is *my* room."

"It's only temporary," Papa said, panting as he struggled to get a folded-up floor mattress through the door. "Oof! Get the bedsheets, will you, sayang?"

"I already have them," Mama said, her arms full of pillows and bedding. "Hurry up lah!"

"Okay, okay." Papa finally got the mattress in, though not without a whole symphony of grunts and groans. "There we go!"

Alia crossed her arms. "*How* temporary?" she asked.

Papa rubbed his head and thought about this. "Well. I have to clear the boxes out of that room downstairs, and then I have to order a bed and a mattress. And the air conditioner in there isn't working either. So maybe . . . a month?"

"A MONTH?"

Mama set the pillows down on top of the mattress and rubbed Alia's shoulders gently. "Maybe this is good," she said softly. "Maybe it's the chance you need to get to know your sister again."

"Or *maybe* she could just sleep on the couch."

"I could." Alia jumped at the sound of Kak Ayu's voice. She was discovering that this girl had a disconcerting habit of just turning up without warning. She walked like a cat; you never heard her coming.

"Don't be silly!" Papa boomed. "There's plenty of room in here, and you girls can talk all night, just like you used to."

"I don't think we have anything to talk about," Alia muttered.

Kak Ayu smiled at her. It looked a little wobbly and unsure around the edges. "It could be fun?"

Alia shrugged. "I guess I don't really have a choice."

Papa clapped them both on the back, so hard that they jerked forward. "My girls! Together again! I'm so happy!" And as he chuckled delightedly, Alia didn't have the heart to tell him how she really felt.

The first thing Alia noticed was the smell.

It wasn't *bad* bad, the way her cousin Afif smelled after he'd been out playing football—that stench could make anyone gag, truly. Kak Ayu sprayed herself with generous amounts of perfume every morning. But beneath the pretty floral scent, Alia could smell something else, something with a sour, metallic edge to it. And it *stuck*. Alia would be sitting in class idly thinking about what she'd eat during recess when she'd suddenly catch a whiff of Kak Ayu's scent and realize it was coming from *her*. And it was horrifying. Nobody, *nobody* wanted to be the smelly kid. *Ever.*

And Kak Ayu was making her the smelly kid.

Yet another reason to not like her.

"You have to admit, it's *weird*," Alia whispered to Mama as they stood side by side in the kitchen, peeling onions and garlic and shallots.

"What is?"

"Where do I *start*?"

"Don't talk that way about your sister."

"Okay, so the smell," Alia said, admiring how quickly Mama managed to get the papery white skins off the garlic bulbs. She didn't add what she was thinking, which was: *Don't call her my sister.* Alia wasn't quite sure how she felt about the word yet. "Haven't you noticed?"

"Can't say that I have," Mama murmured.

"Oh, come on!"

Mama sighed. "Really, Alia. What could possibly—"

"You're telling me you don't smell it?" Alia bent closer to her mother, just in case anybody was listening. "She tries to hide it with all that perfume, but—"

"Well." Mama paused to consider this. "You know, when a kid hits puberty, their body changes and—"

"Mama. Please. Stop." Mama's random talks on the perils of puberty were long and often embarrassing. It was always best to cut her off as soon as possible.

"Anyway." Mama's knife moved up and down smoothly as she chopped the garlic into itty-bitty pieces. "I just want you to know, sayang, that it's perfectly natural to feel uncomfortable or even annoyed at your sister. Allah only knows how many times I wanted to strangle your aunt when we were younger . . ."

"Did you actually do it?" Alia asked eagerly. Her mak su was tall and spent a lot of time lifting weights at the gym; the idea of soft, cozy Mama trying to even reach her neck, much less strangle her, made her giggle.

"Alia!" Mama swatted at her with garlicky hands. "Of course not! I'm just saying, part of sisterhood is growing through these differences. Together. Your bond will be stronger for it."

"Sure," Alia muttered. That was the problem, really. It wasn't just forcing them to share a room. It wasn't just the smell. It was this idea everyone seemed to have that the two of them should be *bonding*. Even Kak Ayu. She couldn't walk into her room without her sister smiling and bombarding her with a million questions and comments: *What are you doing, Alia?* and *Tell me about your friends at school,* and *Gosh, I felt the same way when I was your age.* She couldn't sit down on the couch for five minutes without Mama or Papa gasping theatrically and saying things like "Oh no, we're out of milk! Why don't you and your sister go to the store together to get some?" Like it wasn't the most obvious ploy in the world.

Alia wished she could be rude, that she could just say "Go away," that she could snap "Stop bothering me." But she had spent her whole life from the minute Kak Ayu left trying to be the very best daughter she could. Trying to show her parents that she wasn't like that, that she wouldn't break their hearts. So she wasn't about to hurt their feelings *now*.

Mama smiled at her. "And if the worst you can complain about is a little bit of a smell, well"—Mama shrugged—"then I'd say you're pretty lucky."

Funny, that. The fact that Mama had used the word "lucky." Because if you asked anybody else, if you told them the kinds of things happening to Alia now that her sister was back in her life, that's what you'd say too.

It turned out that Kak Ayu came home with a fully loaded toolbox and an impressive set of cooking skills. That meant she took over preparing their meals, so that they could all stop eating greasy takeout when Mama was busy; and it meant she went around the house doing all the things Papa had always meant to "get around to doing someday, when I have the time." Kak Ayu had the time. Pictures that had spent weeks leaning against walls got hung up; Alia's bathroom door finally stopped squeaking; piles of unopened Ikea boxes magically got turned into the chairs and shelves they were supposed to be.

"You really learned to take care of yourself," Papa said, smiling fondly at the sight of Kak Ayu bent over a sea of furniture parts, Allen key in hand.

"I had no choice," she muttered, then looked up, stricken. "I mean . . . I didn't mean . . ."

Papa stared at her, then nodded. "No, you're right. You had to, after all."

Alia scrunched up her nose. Her eyes felt itchy. Once upon a time, she remembered when a comment like that would've spiraled into an explosive argument. Now it was a Hallmark moment, a cheesy lovey-dovey sitcom special.

And the warm, fuzzy feelings continued—for everyone else. The little gang of students who had been plaguing one of Papa's courses suddenly decided for some reason to stop tormenting him. "They come on time now," he told the family wonderingly over the dinner table. "Early, even. They turn in their assignments. They've stopped trying to give me sassy answers to every question. Sometimes, they even act like they're a little bit scared of me!"

Kak Ayu coughed, and Alia glanced over at her. "Sorry," she croaked. "Choked on my pasta."

"It's called respect, sayang," Mama said, patting

Papa on the arm. "And of course they respect you! You're a fine teacher."

Papa smiled, though it looked a little wobbly at the edges. "I suppose . . ."

Days later, a mysterious package was dropped off at the door of Papa's office, and he opened it to find a puppet he'd been hunting for the longest time, an antique piece from one of wayang kulit's original masters. He didn't stop reverently gloating about it for days. "Who sent this?" he'd asked over and over, poring over every inch of the parcel for some kind of name, or any indication of where it had come from. But there was nothing. Kak Ayu tried to display it, along with all Papa's other puppets, in Instagram-worthy corners of the house. But Papa shot this down.

"Why?" Kak Ayu asked. "Why not show them off? They're beautiful."

"Some things aren't meant to be shown off," Papa told her. "Some things are better kept to yourself."

"But why?" Alia echoed, interested in spite of herself.

"Because." And that was that.

Mama was content too, humming like a delighted bee as she went about her days. Now that she was free from the confines of the kitchen and basic housework, she could pull on her boots and go trekking through the nearby jungle or spend hours looking through carefully preserved fungus samples in the quiet of her office on the top floor of the house. Mama would look over at Kak Ayu, mopping the floor or chopping away in the kitchen, and say things like "Our luck really changed when she came home."

They're so happy, Alia thought. *Why can't you be happy too, Alia?* But no matter how hard she tried, there was a feeling in the pit of her stomach like she'd tried to swallow a piece of gum and it refused to go down. It just hung there, heavy and uncomfortable. She'd been here this whole time, hadn't she? She'd tried so hard to be good. And here was Kak Ayu, and she was nice, and she was perfect, and yet somehow Alia had never hated someone more.

But it was Alia, really, who was luckiest of all. There were whooshes, still, if she paid attention, and the shadows still moved in strange ways sometimes when she looked. It's just that Alia wasn't always looking. She still tripped and slipped and fell as she always did, but somehow things seemed determined to work themselves out, no matter what she did or didn't do about it.

There was the day she happened to sigh about not having money to buy the clay that it seemed like everyone else was buying from the school bookstore and using to make all sorts of Technicolor characters between classes. Alia knew what she'd buy, if she had the money. She'd make a lime-green lizard, with magenta stripes. She'd been thinking about it for days, could see it in her head, feel in her fingers exactly how to make the shapes she needed. She was thinking about it again, hands shoved deep in the pockets of her PE sweatpants, when she felt her fingers graze against something. She grasped it in her hand and pulled out five whole ringgits—enough for two packets of clay and an iced Milo from the canteen too.

Alia smiled. Then she frowned. "Where'd this come from?"

"Who cares?" Raekha, who sat behind her, shook her head. "It was in your pocket. Now you can get that clay and maybe the rest of us can stop hearing about your lizard."

It wasn't until later, when she was waiting for the bookshop auntie to hand her the clay and waving away a particularly persistent mosquito, that she smelled it: a smell that clung to her hand, familiar and faintly sour.

Kak Ayu's smell.

Or the day she'd completely forgotten to finish her maths homework and knew she'd get into trouble for it, except that their teacher never turned up. They learned later that their teacher's brand-new car had randomly broken down on the way to school; she spent an hour waiting for roadside assistance to come and help her.

(Kak Ayu had appeared at the dinner table clean and tidy as usual, except for a mysterious dark stain on her pants.)

Or the day she turned up at school sick with anxiety over having to take an Arabic test she didn't feel at all prepared for, and Ustazah came to class to tell them it was canceled because somehow ink had spilled all over the papers. "They're unreadable," she'd said, shaking her head sadly. "It's just too bad." And the kids had mumbled their agreement.

(This time, the dark stains were beneath Kak Ayu's fingernails. Alia didn't know why she was looking for these things, or what kinds of conclusions she wanted to form from what she saw.)

Or the day Alia was craving a curry chicken pau during Bahasa Melayu class, the ones Papa would buy at the market once he was done shopping for the week.

"They're so big and so fluffy and so soft," she told Charlene dreamily, imagining the pillowy white pau in her hands. "And you bite into them and the chicken inside is still steaming. . . ."

"And you burn your tongue and you give yourself a tummy ache because you ate it too fast," Charlene said. "Why are you dreaming about food you don't have and can't get right now? Faster, let's finish this homework."

Alia sighed. "Fine. But if I have to write another essay about being a pencil, I will eat my own shoe."

"You might as well," Charlene muttered. "Because you're not getting that pau anyway."

But the pau was waiting for her when she got home, sitting in a white paper bag in the center of her desk. Another coincidence. Another piece of luck. Another thing nobody at home could have known about.

Alia walked over to it slowly. When she picked up the bag, her hands were trembling.

It was still warm.

Coincidence, she thought. *Papa must have bought it for me as a treat.*

She took a bite. It was just as good, just as delicious as she remembered. But somehow, she couldn't make herself eat the rest.

6

"You look like you haven't slept at all," Charlene said as she set her container of food on the table and slid onto the bench next to Alia.

"I haven't," Alia mumbled. Her eyes felt swollen from tiredness. She still wasn't used to sharing a room, and Kak Ayu's smell and how eager she was to be kind and helpful and the *closeness* of it all was starting to get to her.

"No, I mean . . . you look terrible. Like really horrendous."

Alia sighed. "I get it, thanks."

Just next to them, there were gales of laughter. "You're so funny, Su Ann," a girl named June gasped, and Su Ann flicked her hair, a look of smug satisfaction on her face.

Alia rolled her eyes. "Why is she always like this?"

She said it quietly, so Su Ann wouldn't hear. The canteen was small, and the teachers always forced them to fill every seat at every table to make sure there was room for everyone. Otherwise, Alia would rather tether herself to a tree with a rope and eat grass like a cow before choosing to sit at the same table as Su Ann and her minions.

"Who?" Charlene asked through a mouthful of fried rice. "Su Ann? As if you don't know that popular kids get away with everything."

"Popularity is such a weird concept," Alia muttered, taking a bite of her tuna sandwich. "How do we just decide one particular person's going to be THE one at the center of the universe, anyway?"

"Why are you acting like this is some weird phenomenon?" Charlene took a sip of water from her bottle. "Your school in KL also had popular kids, right?"

"That's right!" Su Ann spoke up brightly before Alia could answer. "I keep forgetting that Alia moved here allllll the way from Kuala Lumpur!" How did she manage to make even the most innocent sentences sound like insults?

Two seats down, Raekha chewed the end of her long dark braid and wrinkled her nose. "Why would you?" she asked. "I mean . . . there's nothing here. KL is so much cooler."

"There's one thing we have that KL doesn't," June said, grinning. "Hantu!"

Su Ann groaned and sat back, crossing her arms. "Not this again."

"No, really!" June looked around the table, eyes wide. "I swear this is the most haunted town in all of Malaysia."

Su Ann tossed her perfect ponytail. "You're being ridiculous."

Alia frowned and tried to rack her memories, but she couldn't remember ever hearing anything about ghosts back when they'd lived here the first time. "What makes you say that?" she asked.

Beside Alia, a girl named Mastura fidgeted awkwardly. "I mean . . ." she said quietly, and then shrank back a little when all eyes turned to her. "June's got a point," she squeaked. "You can't tell me you haven't noticed some weird things happening around here lately. . . ."

"Like what?" Charlene asked, her mouth full of food.

"Like . . ." June pondered this for a while. "Okay,

like the other day, right, my dad was yelling at us because the TV kept switching itself on, and at, like, top volume every time. He thought it was me and my brother playing a prank on him. But it wasn't." June looked at us, her eyes wide. "We never touched the remote, or the TV. And it just kept doing it."

"So your TV broke," Su Ann said in her most bored voice. "Pull the plug lah. Habis cerita."

"We did," June said quietly. "Then the TV switched itself on again and started blaring the news. Like it was scolding us."

Next to Alia, Charlene shivered. "Spooky," she said. "You need a priest or an exorcist or a ghost-buster or . . ."

"Or an electrician," Su Ann said.

"I thought I was the only one weird things were happening to!" Raekha leaned forward, like she was ready to share some deep, dark secret. "Have you guys been hearing weird whooshing sounds too? Like something's flying by really fast?"

As other voices chimed in (OMG, *what? Me too! I thought it was just me!*), Alia's heart dropped all the way down to her brand-new shoes. *Whooshes and shadows . . .*

"I don't hear anything," Mastura said. "But once I

couldn't sleep late at night, and I looked out the window, and I saw . . . I saw . . ." she hesitated, and Su Ann sighed.

"Spit it out!" she snapped. "Recess is almost over!"

"I saw something flying around outside," Mastura said.

Everyone stared at her. "Well?" June asked. "What was it?"

Mastura gulped and fiddled with the hem of her hijab. "Something. A dark shape. Just flying around in the air . . ."

"That's it?" Su Ann rolled her eyes. "You guys are soooo gullible. That could be anything. A bird, or a drone . . ."

"Or a UFO!" Raekha said helpfully.

"Or a penanggalan!" a girl named Liyana supplied eagerly.

Alia frowned. "What's that?" she asked.

"You don't know?" Liyana's eyes gleamed. "A penanggalan's this terrifying monster that can, like, take off their head and just fly around without their body—"

Before Liyana could go on, Su Ann stood up and sighed loudly. "Who *cares*? You're all *way* too old to believe in kiddie horror stories." She grabbed her things. "I'm going to the hall to wait for the bell. Let me know when you have stories actually worth hearing." Then she sashayed off, her minions trailing along in her wake as usual.

Mastura waited until everyone else had gone before she finally looked up. "I know what I saw," she said softly. "And it wasn't some silly drone." Then she too was gone.

Alia shivered.

She looked over at Charlene, who still sat munching her fried rice without a care in the world. "Do you believe all that?"

Charlene chewed thoughtfully. "No," she said finally. "But that doesn't mean I won't be careful."

"Why?" Alia frowned. "Why be careful, if you don't believe in ghosts and monsters and aliens?"

"Because." Charlene shrugged. "It's like my ma always says. No harm taking extra care, whatever it is. Just because you don't believe in them, doesn't mean they don't believe in *you*."

7

The next day, Alia spent a good ten minutes rummaging frantically through her backpack for the history homework that was due that afternoon, until she forced herself to accept the fact that she'd forgotten it.

"Figures," Su Ann said, smirking at Alia from where she sat two seats away. "You're always forgetting things. Puan Aminah is going to *murder* you."

Alia kept riffling through her books, checking between each page even though she knew the homework wasn't there. "I know." The gathering storm clouds outside matched her feelings perfectly.

"She already told you. The last time you forgot that worksheet. Remember? *I consider myself a patient person, Nur Alia, but your forgetfulness would test the patience of a thousand saints combined . . .*"

"I *know*," Alia snapped. "You don't have to remind me."

"Clearly someone should," Su Ann said, lips curled into a sneer. "Then maybe you could go, like, two days without getting into trouble. But what else can we expect from the daughter of the town's original absent-minded professors?"

Hushed giggles went around the room, and Alia clenched her hands into tight fists. "Stop it," she said, heart pounding in her ears. "Don't talk about my parents like that."

"Calm down, girls," snapped class monitor Farah as she walked over to flick on the switch. Light flooded the darkened room. Outside, thunder groaned ominously. "The teacher'll be here soon. No more fighting."

"Give it up, Alia," Su Ann said, rolling her eyes, as if Farah hadn't even spoken. "Your family is weird and we all know it. Your mom's obsessed with mushrooms—"

"Fungi," Alia supplied automatically. Su Ann kept talking as if she didn't even notice.

"And your dad had puppets all over the house back then. Puppets! You can't tell me that's not, like, deeply strange. And *creepy*. I bet he still has them *now*."

"They're for his *research*!"

Su Ann tossed her perfect ponytail. "And now my mom says your sister is back! Of all things!"

"Sister?" Charlene stared at Alia. "I didn't even know you had a sister. . . ."

"I didn't. I mean. It's not." Alia's cheeks felt red-hot, and the words just wouldn't come out the way she meant them to. She'd thought now and then about what she'd do if Su Ann brought up the past. She'd just never considered that this was the part Su Ann would bring up.

"Of course she does!" Su Ann tilted her chair back on two legs, grinning widely. "I should know. I was there. Remember, Alia?" Her smile had the kind of hungry glee that a cat gets when it's looking at a trapped mouse.

"Remember what?"

"Well." Su Ann flipped that long, perfect ponytail. "Remember your sister running away, silly."

"How would you even know about that?" Charlene's face was all creased with confusion.

"Because I lived next door." Su Ann grinned at Alia. "And because we were *besties*."

Charlene gaped at Alia. "Is that *true*?"

Before Alia could answer, Farah spoke.

"What's that sound?"

They all quieted down to hear it, a low buzzing that seemed to be coming from above their heads. The lights flickered as they watched, and Alia felt her blood turn to ice in her veins.

The classroom was dead silent now except for the buzzing, an electrical hum that swelled and grew until it was so loud that it made them cover their ears and grit their teeth.

"What's happening?" Su Ann yelled.

At that exact moment, every single lightbulb in the class exploded.

Alia ducked beneath her desk, heart pounding, as the classroom filled with the sounds of panicked screams and shrieks. "What's going on?" "Oh my god!" "Someone get a teacher!"

Farah stood up, shoes crunching sickeningly against broken glass. "Everyone stay calm!" she said, and her voice, so loud, so steady, felt like an anchor to cling on to. "Whatever's happening, it looks like it's stopped. Let's get out of here and we'll figure out what to—"

Hurried footsteps pounded down the hallway. "Girls? Girls? What happened here—ya Allah!" Puan Aminah stared, mouth wide open, at the scene before her. "Okay, come out of there! Come out! Don't touch anything, you'll get cut, nanti. Ya Allah, what happened here?"

Slowly, the girls made their way out, gingerly stepping over bits of glass. "Are you okay?" Charlene asked Alia quietly.

"Ya, why?"

Charlene gestured to Alia's arm, where a stray piece of glass must have gashed a thin red line from the base of her thumb down to her wrist.

"I'm fine," Alia said quickly. It was only then that she realized how much it hurt.

Eventually, once they'd checked everything to make sure it was safe, the teachers got them to file back into the room. Most of the glass had been swept up, but bits and pieces remained, and the girls did their best to comb the room for even the tiniest shards.

"Oh." Alia paused when she got back to her desk. Because there, sticking slightly out of her sejarah textbook, was Alia's history homework.

"How did you miss that?" Charlene picked a tiny bit of glass off the corner of her desk and wrapped it carefully in the paper towels their teacher had handed out. "My mom would say your mata are on your bontot, you know."

"My eyes are not on my butt," Alia mumbled. She could've sworn she'd already looked through her textbook. . . .

"Anyway, good lah. Now you won't get into trouble!"

"Mm-hmm." Alia nodded slowly. "I guess not."

There was a gasp. From beneath her desk, Su Ann straightened, staring at her cupped palms. Nestled within them was what looked like a mound of . . .

"What is it?" Liyana asked.

"Confetti?" Alia suggested, frowning.

Su Ann shook her head. "No. It's . . . it's . . ."

Farah sighed. "What?"

"It's my history homework." Su Ann swallowed hard. Alia could have sworn it looked like she was trying not to cry, and the thought made her insides squirm. "It's been ripped to pieces."

For the rest of the day, all Alia could think about were whooshes and swooshes, good luck and coincidences, bad luck and broken glass, homework ruined and homework found, and a thin red scar that still stung.

She wasn't scared, exactly, she told herself as she walked home from the bus stop, kicking at rocks as she went. It was just this nagging feeling that there was something she wasn't quite seeing. Something to do with her sister, and the way there was always something that seemed to tie her to Alia's good luck.

Alia shook her head. *You're being silly.*

But.

But. It was like a worm that had dug its way into her brain and stayed there, squirming.

But how is she always there? *And how does she always* know? *And why do all the things that have happened to you feel like they were personally done just for you? And how many coincidences does it take until you start drawing some inevitable conclusions?*

Alia stopped in her tracks. *And what conclusion are you trying to draw exactly, Alia? That your sister is some kind of alien? Some kind of monster?*

Ridiculous. She was being ridiculous over a bunch of nothing. She'd been haunted by bad luck long enough, hadn't she? It was time for good things to happen to her for once. That was all. The universe swinging back into balance.

But.

It was such a tiny little word, and it just refused to leave her alone.

But maybe keep an eye on her? said the little voice in her head. *Just in case.*

Alia kicked at another rock and almost slipped.

Behind her, there was a quiet little *whoosh*, like the sound of something flying through the air.

Alia thought about new shoes and hot pau and miraculously reappearing homework and stains on pants and dirt under fingernails. Her heart pounded so hard, it echoed in her ears.

How does she always know? Alia thought. *How does she always know what to do? What we need?*

Was it just Alia, or was there a faint, sour scent in the air?

There was nobody else around; the house was in sight, but still too far away for anyone to see her. She took another step, then another. *Get a grip, Alia.*

Just ahead, the sidewalk bulged and cracked where a tree root had pushed its way through. It only took a split second for her foot to catch on its crooked tangles. She fell hard, pain blossoming from her knees and skinned palms. The sting, along with the tiny drops of blood oozing from the cuts, made her wince. "Oh man," she said aloud. "What bad luck."

The leaves rustled, even though there was no wind.

Alia hauled herself back to her feet and headed home. She walked slowly up the stairs to her room and paused to take a deep breath before opening her door.

There, lined up perfectly in the center of her desk, was a box of Band-Aids, brand-new and unopened, for all the world as if it had been waiting for her all along.

"Alia!" Mama called from downstairs. "Ayu! Come and help me put away these groceries!"

"Coming!" Alia yelled back. There was no time to dwell on the Band-Aids, or think about what they meant. She walked downstairs, wincing at the way her knee stung, only to have Mama brush right past her in a hurry at the bottom of the stairs.

"I need the bathroom," she called over her shoulder. "The things are in the car."

Slowly, Alia slid her feet into her sandals and walked over to the car. The back door had been flung open, and bags full of groceries lined the seat like sentinels. She was just about to grab the nearest handle when someone pushed her aside. "I'll do it," Kak Ayu said.

"Mama told me to help."

"Just let me." Kak Ayu hauled two of the bags out of the car. "You just hurt your kn—I mean." She cleared her throat and gestured to Alia's arm with a nod of her head. "Your hand."

Alia looked down at the scratch on her hand, and frowned. "Were you . . . were you going to say something else?"

"No." Kak Ayu walked past, a bag in each hand, not looking Alia in the eye. "Now go get some rest while I put these away. Don't forget to solat."

Knee, Alia thought to herself. *She was going to say, you just hurt your knee*. And the thought made her want to throw up.

Because how could Kak Ayu know that unless she was there?

9

She's spying on me.

The words went round and round in Alia's head, like the spinning tea cup ride that had made her barf that time they went to Disneyland. *I don't know how, but she's spying on me.* There was no other explanation, no way she could know everything that she knew. The more Alia thought about it, the angrier she got. And the angrier she got, the better she felt, because it was so much better to be angry than to be scared.

"Our luck really changed when she came home," her mother had said.

So it wasn't luck after all, was it? It was her disgraced sister, following them around like a little sneak and using all that she saw and heard to worm her way into their lives. And specifically, into Alia's good graces.

But how? Just how was Kak Ayu able to be everywhere, all at once?

Maths wasn't exactly Alia's best subject, but you didn't need to be a genius to know that something wasn't adding up.

That night, Alia lay awake, staring up at the ceiling. The window was open; the room was small, and two bodies made it far too stuffy to keep it closed. On the floor, a sliver of moonlight peeked through the curtains and sliced sharply across her sister's sleeping form.

Alia didn't sleep. She was keeping watch.

Alia tried to remember what Kak Ayu had been like before, but the memories came to her only in bits and pieces: tickle fights; Kak Long's gentle fingers weaving Alia's long hair into all sorts of complicated styles every morning before she left for school; bedtime stories under the covers (*Just one more, Kak Long, please, please, pretty please with a cherry on top*); the way Kak Long's hands felt against her back as she pushed Alia on the swings (*Higher, Kak Long, higher!*); Mama and Papa talking in low voices behind closed doors late into the night, her mother's voice gentle, coaxing (*It's just growing pains, sayang . . .*), her father's a growl (*More like a growing pain in the you-know-where*); the way Alia would wake every night in tears from confused dreams of slamming doors and being left, over and over and over again; waiting by the window every day, keeping vigil, watching for her to walk back up the path and open the door as if nothing had happened (*She's coming home soon, Mama. I just know it*).

No, she didn't want to think about that.

The night air was hot and still, and a lone mosquito kept buzzing in her ear right as she was about to doze off. On the floor, Kak Ayu snored gently. Alia couldn't tell if she was more irritated by her sister's peaceful slumber or her own brilliant plan to deprive herself of precious sleep in order to see if said sister would . . . she wasn't even sure what. Get up and start spying on them? She pictured Kak Ayu in a brown trench coat and fedora, a giant magnifying glass in one hand, and snorted.

Nothing about this makes sense, Alia thought to herself sourly. She rolled over and shut her eyes tight, trying to ignore the mosquito that still hovered persistently around her head. *Go to sleep, Alia. You'll laugh about this in the morning. You'll—*

Squelch.

It was a sticky, oozy kind of sound, as if someone had gotten their shoe stuck in thick mud and was having trouble getting it out. It was not a sound one expected to hear in the middle of the night, in a house, with no mud in sight. And as she listened to it, Alia felt every single hair on her arms stand on end.

Behind her, Kak Ayu groaned softly.

Turn around, Alia. You stayed up for this. You wanted to know. You wanted to be sure.

So she turned around. And let out a horrified yelp.

Because Kak Ayu's head was on backward.

Backward.

Alia blinked and rubbed her eyes. It might be the middle of the night, but the streetlights outside meant that dim light straggled in weakly through the window, and there was no denying what she saw. Kak Ayu's body was still curled up facing away from her. But her entire head was turned to look right at Alia, blinking sleepily.

"What is it?" she mumbled.

"I . . . you . . . what . . . ," Alia stammered.

"What?"

"Your HEAD!" Alia's heart was pounding way faster than was healthy. "What's wrong with your HEAD?"

"My head?" Kak Ayu leapt up and Alia shrieked. There was something uniquely terrifying about seeing her sister's puzzled face staring at her while every other part of her was turned the other way. "Here, let me—" She tried to come closer, but apparently the current arrangement of her parts hadn't quite sunk in yet, so that in walking forward, she actually walked *away* from Alia, and then squealed when she bumped her leg on a corner of the desk.

"No, stay away! Stay away from me!" Alia clutched at her bed desperately. She thought she might throw up.

"Alia? Ayu?" There was a click and Alia blinked as bright light suddenly flooded the room. "What's going on?" Papa asked grumpily, his sarong hanging askew around his waist.

"I think Alia had a nightmare," Kak Ayu said.

"I did not!" Alia bristled. She turned to her father. "It's just that her head—"

"What about it?" Papa asked, frowning.

"Well, can't you see, Papa? It's . . . it's . . ." Alia whirled around to point at Kak Ayu's head.

Which was facing the same way as the rest of her body, just as regular heads did.

"It looks fine to me," Papa said.

"Which is more than I can say for my leg." Kak Ayu rubbed her thigh ruefully. "Alia must have had a nightmare and woken up when I bumped up against the desk, Papa." She flashed Alia an apologetic smile. "I was just trying to get my bottle; it's so hot, I really needed a drink. Sorry."

"But . . . but . . ." Alia stared at Kak Ayu's head in disbelief. "It was . . . I swear it was . . ."

"Could you stop staring?" Kak Ayu said, pulling at her shirt collar. A pink blush stained her cheeks. "You're making me self-conscious."

Alia turned to her father desperately. "Papa . . ."

But Papa was already heading out the door. "Go to bed, girls," he grumbled over his shoulder. "Or I'll give your heads something to worry about."

Alia and Kak Ayu crawled back under their respective blankets and turned out the lights. But for the rest of the night, Alia did nothing but stare at the shape on the floor, watching and wary and desperately reciting Ayat Kursi over and over again. She knew what she saw, and it could only mean one thing.

There was something wrong with her sister.

10

When Alia woke up, she sat bolt upright in bed. The mattress on the floor was rolled up in the corner, pillows and neatly folded blanket stacked on top. In the sunlit warmth of a new morning, it was hard to remember what exactly she'd been so afraid of.

At breakfast, Mama cleared her throat. "We thought it might be best if Ayu slept downstairs instead," she said. "Give you girls your own space. You know. While we all adjust." Kak Ayu nodded, scratching at her neck, and Alia munched her cereal and tried not to give away just how relieved she felt.

As she made her way through the familiar motions of the day, the feelings of the night before slowly became more and more unreal. *You must have been imagining it, Alia. Had some kind of nightmare. How can a head be on backward? Be reasonable.*

The thing is, at any other time, Alia would probably have let this go. She'd have told herself to stop being ridiculous, and to get over it. Eventually, she and Kak Ayu might even have ended up becoming friends. Maybe. And maybe they would laugh together someday about the time Alia thought her sister somehow had her head on backward.

Maybe.

But.

The word just wouldn't leave her alone. *But what about the fact that she's watching you, prying into your life without your permission? What about the fact that she doesn't seem to care whether someone else has a hard time as long as you don't? What about leaving a teacher stranded, adding hours to another's workload? What about the pieces of Su Ann's homework, scattered all over the floor? What about the head, Alia? What about the head?*

The thoughts swarmed all over her mind like tiny little ants and made her restless and uneasy. She did her best to avoid her sister after school, mumbling something about all the homework she had to do before escaping to her room. Even still, she was wrestling with maths when a shadow fell across her book, and she looked up to see her sister smiling timidly at her. That smell, that faintly sour scent, hit her nostrils before she even realized Kak Ayu was there. Alia couldn't help it; she inched toward the farthest edge of her desk, as far away from Kak Ayu as she could.

"What?"

"Come on," Kak Ayu said, reaching out a hand.

Alia stared at it, then at her. "Come on where?"

"It's Tuesday," Kak Ayu said simply. "Where else?"

Alia's hands clenched themselves into tight fists. The pages of the exercise book she was holding crumpled beneath her grip. *Mrs. Sumathi is going to kill me if I rip this paper.* But somehow she couldn't make herself unclench. "So?"

"So . . ." Kak Ayu wavered, uncertain, her other hand fiddling with the scarf around her neck as usual. Alia tried very hard not to focus on that neck, tried very hard not to remember that sickening, wet squelch. "So . . . shall we go to the playground?"

Alia paused. What she thought was: *How dare she? How dare she act like nothing happened?* And, somewhere further back, in a darker place of her mind that she tried not to acknowledge: *And what will she do to me if I say no?*

What she said was: "I'm too old for playgrounds." Alia turned her attention back to her book, ignoring

71

the way Kak Ayu's hand trembled for an instant in the air before she snatched it back. Her face felt like it was burning. She wished the smell would go away. She wished Kak Ayu would too.

"Oh," Kak Ayu said. "Okay." She started to walk out the door, then paused, one hand on the doorknob. "You know, Alia," she said, her voice low. "I've done nothing but be nice to you. I know having me just turn up like this is really disruptive for you. All I've been doing is trying to make your life a little easier, show you how much I care. Is that not enough for you?"

If Alia buried her face any farther into her book, she'd end up with math equations imprinted on her forehead. Her throat was dry. She didn't say a word.

"Fine." Kak Ayu drew herself up straight and tall. "Fine. If that's how you want to play it, go right ahead. But don't blame me if your life gets a little harder now that you've decided I'm the enemy." And with that, she yanked open the door and left.

Alia went back to her homework, to a world where every question had to have an answer that made sense. She tried not to notice the way her hands shook.

Alia spent a lot of time thinking about how exactly Kak Ayu planned to make her life harder. Well, not just thinking. Also worrying. And stressing. And imagining dozens of terrible scenarios that somehow all ended with her parents banishing her from the house while her sister stood behind them, arms folded, a smug expression on her face. *I told you so*, imaginary Kak Ayu said every time. *I told you not to make me your enemy.*

Going to school was almost a relief. It was the one place Kak Ayu wasn't, after all.

Until she was.

It started, as things so often do these days, with an Instagram post.

None of them were allowed to bring their phones to school, of course. But still, it was all everyone could talk about. Someone had taken a picture, blurry and unrecognizable, of a sort-of roundish thing, outlined against the pale face of the moon. *Look at this!!!* the tweet said. *I couldn't sleep the other night and glanced out my window and this weird thing was zooming around in the sky!! What do you think it is???*

Alia didn't have an Instagram account—it was one of those things her mother thought of as junk food for kid brains—but suddenly *everyone* was obsessed with trying to figure out what the Thing was. Speculation ranged from "It's a UFO!" to "Clean your camera lens; it's just a speck of dust," and everything in between.

Some people insisted it was just a bat that was out of focus; a small but vocal contingent decided it was a falling meteor and vigorously insulted anyone who disagreed.

But Liyana tapped her forehead knowingly. "Penanggalan," she said. "I'm telling you. That's what it is."

Alia thought of her sister, head all twisted around in the wrongest of ways, and shivered. "Do you think she could be right?" she whispered to Charlene.

Charlene blinked. "No," she said bluntly. "I told you. I'm team UFO. I even made a list of bullet points about why I think it's aliens! Wanna see?"

"Maybe later." Alia slumped over her desk. She'd never been so willing to believe in aliens until right this minute.

Unfortunately for Alia, the alien theory didn't last very long. Not even two days later, a girl named Auni came to school and told as many people as she could that she and her brother had stayed up all night to try and catch sight of the speck, and they *had*, and they *knew what it was*. "And," she whispered to an excited group of girls, "we have *proof*."

June tossed her hair in a poor imitation of Su Ann's signature move, which made Su Ann herself roll her eyes. "Sure or not?"

Auni bristled. "Of course lah!"

"Show us, then."

Auni looked around, then slowly drew a phone out from beneath her voluminous school hijab.

There was a quiet gasp. "You know we're not allowed to bring phones to school!" Misha, who was a prefect, looked visibly nervous. "I'm going to have to confiscate it . . ."

"Let her show us first lah, at least!" Su Ann hissed. She'd done her best to look bored and disinterested before this, but now she was as eager as the rest to see what Auni had to show them.

"I got video," Auni announced softly. "If you take my phone, you won't be able to see it."

Misha wavered for only a moment or two. "Come on, Mishaaaaa," some of the girls began to whine.

She sighed. "Okay fine. Show us first."

The girls drew closer as Auni swiped through her gallery and hit play.

Alia held her breath.

The video shuddered and jerked, held in shaking hands. All you could hear was heavy breathing and the sound of a male voice—Auni's brother, Alia assumed—saying "Ya Allah!" over and over again under his breath. But eventually, as Auni steadied herself long enough to focus on a point between the bars they seemed to be crouched behind ("That's our balcony," she explained breathlessly to the watching girls. "We live in a condo"), the camera focused just long enough for everyone to see it clearly: a head, hair streaming behind it in the wind, entrails flapping below.

The video ended. For one brief moment, it was like everyone held their breath.

And then Mastura stood up at her desk. "I TOLD you!" she said triumphantly. "I TOLD you I saw something!"

Immediately, the whole class plunged into chaos.

"What is that?"

"Oh my god!"

"It's the penanggalan!" Liyana crowed, shooting a look at Su Ann. "That's what it is! Just like I said it was."

Su Ann just bit her lip and said nothing.

"That is so. *Scary!*"

Auni sat back, smug and victorious at being the cause of all this chaos, and Alia sank into her seat.

"Who do we tell? What can we do?" Charlene fanned herself, her face pale.

"What if it *eats us*?"

"It might," Liyana said solemnly. "Penanggalan don't just eat *whatever*. They detach their heads from their bodies, and then go flying around with their entrails dangling, looking for babies and, like, little kids. And some of us—" she shot a look at Mastura, the shortest among them, and the girl's face went deathly pale. "Some of us are, um. Littler than others."

"Babies and kids?" Alia gulped. "What do they want with babies and kids?"

"Because that's what they eat, of course," Liyana said matter-of-factly.

"That's not what I heard," June said. "My grandma says they drink blood. Especially the blood that comes out of a woman after they've just had babies. And if the penanggalan gets a taste of that blood, the woman dies. My grandma said she saw it happen herself, in her kampung last time. And then it has to soak its body in vinegar, so that when the head flies back, the organs left inside the body shrink up enough so that it can easily fit its head and entrails and stuff back on when it flies back."

Vinegar. Alia thought of the faintly sour smell that clung to her sister and anything she touched. Her head was spinning.

Liyana frowned. "No, no, it's definitely babies and children the penanggalan wants. And she uses her entrails to reach through open windows or through floorboards and snatch them away in the dead of night. And what's up with the vinegar thing?" Liyana snorted. "It's a penanggalan, not a pickle."

June stuck her bottom lip out mutinously. "But my grandma said—"

Liyana shrugged. "Well. I guess some people hear different stories." Something in her tone implied that June's grandmother was simply wrong, but she was too polite to say so.

"What does it matter, anyway?" Mastura said. "As long as you pray and read the correct doas . . ."

"Does that mean nonreligious people just have to *deal with it?*" Raekha shrieked, and the whole class began to debate loudly about what one could do to protect themself from the supernatural.

Alia paid no attention to them. Her mind was going at two hundred kilometers an hour, and she couldn't make it stop. Kak Ayu's head, turned all the way around to look at her. Kak Ayu, always knowing things she couldn't possibly know. Kak Ayu, trailing that sour smell everywhere she went.

Was this real? Was it true? Was that Kak Ayu? And if it was, what would happen? It was only a matter of time before someone got hurt, or eaten, or people figured out that Ayu was Alia's sister, and that her parents had unknowingly invited a penanggalan to their neighborhood, to their town, to live among them. It was only a matter of time before she ruined the life Alia was trying to build for herself—again— and scarred her parents beyond measure. *Again.*

"Are you okay?" Charlene whispered, and Alia realized she was gripping the edge of the table so tight, her knuckles were white.

"Fine," she said, attempting a smile. "I'm just fine."

There was no point getting lost in what-ifs. Alia sat quietly as the girls continued chattering all around her, and forced herself to think. *Be rational, Alia. It's not like I really believe she's a penanggalan.* She drummed her fingers on her table. It was hard to keep still. *But the video, and all the signs . . .*

The bell rang, and somehow she managed to stand on her two shaky legs, along with everyone else. *There's only one way to be sure*, she thought to herself. *I'm just going to have to prove that Kak Ayu is a penanggalan, once and for all.*

Before it's too late.

11

From that moment on, Alia had only one goal: to watch her sister like a hawk hunting prey.

Fortunately, keeping watch wasn't difficult, because Kak Ayu didn't really go anywhere. When she wasn't helping around the house (*or spying on me, or magically making all our dreams come true, like some kind of Scary Godmother*, Alia thought sourly), she spent most of her time sitting in front of an ancient laptop in the living room, tapping away at the keys and sighing as she tried to look for a job. "I have to," she told Mama and Papa. "I can't rely on you guys forever. I want to start taking care of you too. The way you're taking care of me." Papa had cleared his throat a lot and looked away all embarrassed, and Mama had patted Ayu's head, teary-eyed and smiling, and Alia had felt like throwing up.

So Alia stationed herself on the couch with a book and tried to remember to turn the pages once in a while so it would at least look like she was reading. But all the while, over the top of the book, she observed her sister, like she was a specimen in a lab and Alia was a scientist about to make a breakthrough discovery.

"What are you doing here?" Kak Ayu asked, and Alia nearly screamed. She hadn't realized her sister was watching her.

"Oh. Um." She held up the book in her hand. "Reading."

"Yeah, I can see that." Kak Ayu tapped her foot impatiently. "But why are you doing it *here?*"

Alia supposed she had a point. Kak Ayu had been avoiding her ever since they had their last conversation. She was still perfectly polite—especially in front of their parents—but it was like there was a word limit she was trying to stick to when it came to speaking to Alia.

"It's not your room, you know," Alia shot back. "I live here too. I have just as much of a right to be here as you."

"It's *practically* my room, since *Princess Alia* decided she didn't want to share," Kak Ayu muttered, her eyes fixed to the screen.

"Excuse you!" Alia almost forgot about the whole sister-being-a-monster thing, so focused was she on sister-being-annoying instead.

"Excuse yourself." Kak Ayu glanced at her and rolled her eyes. "As if anyone would believe the fact that you're reading *Great Expectations*, of all things."

"Why not?" Alia bristled at this, never mind the fact that she'd grabbed the book off the stack Mama kept on the side table, the stack she swore she'd get around to reading "someday." Alia had been forced to swipe off an inch of dust before she could even turn a page without sneezing. "It's a great book," she said firmly. "I'm really enjoying it so far."

"Oh yeah?" Kak Ayu leaned back in her seat. "What's it about?"

"It's about . . ." Alia tried to sneak a look at the back cover without being too obvious. "Pi . . . Pip! Yeah! And how he . . . um . . . expects . . . things . . . to be . . . great . . ."

"All right, girls!" Mama practically twirled into the room, her arms filled with boxes. Alia almost sagged with relief. "It's time!"

Kak Ayu blinked. "For what?"

"Time for some family time, of course!" Papa boomed as he walked in. "It's a board game showdown. Who's ready?" He made air horn noises as Mama whooped and pumped her fists. The embarrassment was almost enough to make Alia forget her fear. Almost.

"Well?" Papa glanced at the two girls, who hadn't moved at all from their seats. "Come on! We've got them all: Snakes and Ladders, Scrabble, Sahibba, Uno, Clue, Risk, Monopoly . . ."

"Not Monopoly," Mama said seriously. "We promised we would never go down that road again. We didn't speak to each other for a week last time."

"You're right," Papa said, nodding gravely. "Best not to take any chances. So, what'll it be, girls?"

She didn't mean to, but somehow Alia found herself exchanging glances with Kak Ayu. And she hated how much it made her heart skip with happiness, this feeling of looking meaningfully at a sibling and having them understand exactly what you were feeling. It had been so long. . . .

"Snakes and Ladders," she said, and Kak Ayu sighed. "Fine."

"It's ON!" Papa yelled, and they both winced.

"Papa . . . softer lah a bit . . ." Kak Ayu said.

He ignored her. "You're going DOWN," he said, crossing his arms, a smug look on his face. "Down . . . some SNAKES."

"Can we at least keep the jokes to a minimum?" Alia murmured as she took her spot around the coffee table, where Mama was busy setting up the game.

"Speaking of jokes." Papa cleared his throat and exchanged knowing glances with Mama. "We need to talk, Alia."

"Hmm?" Alia frowned. "What do you mean?"

"I enjoy pranks as much as the next dad, sayang, but really, messing with my mother's picture is a little bit much. Maybe dial it back down a little."

Alia stared at him. "What are you talking about, Papa?"

"You know." He shrugged. "The picture of your late nenek I keep on my bedside table. You drew on her face. Little scribbles here and there." Papa took a deep breath. "I don't have very many pictures of her. . . . It's very disrespectful, Alia."

"But I . . . I . . ." Now Alia thought she might understand what a mouse caught in a trap might feel like.

"Whoever is doing whatever," Mama cut in, "please leave me out of it. You know I told you all never to touch my things. My office is off-limits, and you going in there despite my asking nicely and messing up my notes and books really disrupts my research and writing process." Mama shook her head disapprovingly.

"I'm really disappointed in you. Whoever it is." But her eyes flickered over to Alia as she spoke.

"It wasn't me!" Alia said. "I didn't do anything!" She could feel tears rising in her throat, and it was making her even angrier. Alia *hated* crying.

Kak Ayu just sat quietly, eyes fixed on the game. But for a brief moment she looked up to meet Alia's gaze.

And smirked.

Don't blame me if your life gets a little harder now that you've decided I'm the enemy.

She did this.

Anger leapt up like flames in Alia's chest. *How dare she*, Alia thought. *How dare she pretend to be so perfect? How dare she pretend like she isn't hiding something? Like this wasn't all her?*

"How could you possibly think I would do any of that?" Alia's voice trembled. She was angry at the monster, but if she was honest with herself, she was just as angry at her parents. *She* was the one who had been here this whole time. *She* was the one trying so hard, for them. *She* was the one who never left. How could they not believe her? How could they not know her better than that?

"Calm down, Alia," Papa said. "Like I said, no harm

to these little tricks. You just have to know when to stop."

Alia got to her feet. "I'll stop right now," she said. It was hard to keep her voice from shaking. "I don't want to play."

"Don't be silly, Alia dear," Mama said. "Go and cut some fruits, will you? Auntie Joyce sent over some nice pears the other day."

Alia wavered. Part of her wanted to yell and scream, break something. Part of her wanted to make sure she did what her parents wanted her to do.

The second part won. Alia walked slowly into the kitchen. She'd never felt less like playing a game in her whole life.

The cutting board and a nice, sharp knife sat waiting for her on the counter. Next to them were the pears, skin still glistening from the thorough rinsing Mama had given them earlier.

Alia gritted her teeth and picked up the knife. Slowly, she sliced away at the pear, juices dripping out onto the board. She tried her best to focus, tried her best not to think about Kak Ayu's smirk, and her parents' accusations. *The pear, Alia. Just think about the pear.*

"Careful." Kak Ayu's voice, when it came, was right

behind her, and Alia jumped. The knife slipped, slicing into human flesh instead of pear. Bright red blood oozed from the fresh cut and dripped onto the board, seeping into the fruit's pale insides.

There was a loud clatter as the knife fell out of Alia's fingers onto the floor. "Apa tu?" Mama yelled from the living room.

"Oh," Alia breathed, pain shooting from her finger.

"Oh," Kak Ayu repeated behind her, and something low and urgent in her tone made the hair on the back of Alia's neck stand on end. She turned slowly, heart pounding, half-afraid of what she might see . . .

. . . which was Kak Ayu, hands clenched into tight fists, tense as a lion waiting to spring, staring, not at Alia, but the blood that still dripped freely from the gash on her finger, her eyes wide and dark and swirling with desperation and longing.

Alia grabbed a kitchen towel and wrapped it quickly around her finger, soaking up the blood and hiding it from view, as Mama fussed around her. "Aiya, cepat, let me see? Is it deep? Do you need stitches?"

"No, Mama, I'm fine," Alia said, her eyes still glued to her sister's face.

"We need the Band-Aids, where are the

Band-Aids. . . ." Mama started scrabbling away at random drawers.

"I'm just . . . going to . . ." Kak Ayu muttered hurriedly as she backed away, then turned and walked out of the room, never even finishing her sentence.

"Hold out your finger."

"What?" Alia blinked at Mama.

Mama clicked her tongue impatiently. "Alia, give me your finger. Cepat."

Alia obeyed, but she couldn't help how badly she was shaking. She had gotten a good look at her sister's face, and the expression she saw there chased away all her rage and replaced it with nothing but ice-cold fear.

Because it had looked a whole lot like hunger.

12

There's a monster living in my house.

Alia had her doubts before, but now there wasn't a single one left. Not when she thought about the strange way Ayu's neck moved, the way she'd seen her head on backward, the hunger she'd glimpsed in those dark eyes at the sight of blood. And she knew that she had to tell her parents, before Kak Ayu did something that hurt either of them—both literally and figuratively. But Alia knew Mama and Papa, and she knew they'd never believe her unless they saw solid, irrefutable proof.

So how was she going to get it?

Not for the first time, she wished she had a friend to talk to about these kinds of things. Charlene was nice, but she wasn't really the type of friend you could just call and say "Hey, I think my sister's a monster who takes off her head and eats babies. You wanna come over and help me with that?" That, Alia figured, was a level of friendship that probably took more than a few recess times together to unlock. And Mama and Papa were so thrilled their beloved daughter was back, they weren't going to listen to her until she had actual evidence.

So, until you've got it, you're on your own, Alia.

Step one: know your enemy.

In every movie Alia had ever seen and every book she'd ever read, the heroes only figured out how to beat the villains after learning as much about them as they could. Frodo talked to Gandalf. Luke talked to Obi-Wan. Moana talked to her grandma. Everyone had an oracle, someone to show them The Way.

And that's why, when Alia rolled up to school the next day, she knew exactly what she needed to do: talk to Liyana. She was the one who knew everything penanggalan, right? She was the one who'd have the answers.

Her chance came during PE, when they were being forced to practice for Sports Day. "High jumps, long jumps and footraces!" Mr. Simon announced cheerfully at the start of the period, and all the girls groaned.

Between jumps, Alia noticed Liyana slip away to the canteen, and quickly followed. She found the other girl sipping on a plastic bag of ice-cold grape juice, sweat soaking through her green T-shirt.

"Hey," Alia said, sitting beside her. Act natural, Alia.

"Hi." Liyana sucked up more of the unnaturally purple liquid, panting slightly. "Did you see me out there? I ran so fast."

"Did you?" Alia murmured. She wondered how she was going to turn the conversation away from sports and toward supernatural shenanigans.

"Um, yeah." Liyana mopped up some sweat with the sleeve of her shirt. "I was like the Flash, okay? All the other girls ever saw was my back." She stretched her arms up high, all smug satisfaction. "There's no way I won't be winning some gold medals on Sports Day. I was just too far ahead—"

"Hey, speaking of heads!" *Nice one, Alia, very smooth.* "Remember the stuff we were talking about the other day? Those headless hantus? What were they called again?" It was tricky, this whole pretending business. "Pembaris? Penyapu?"

"You mean penanggalan?" Liyana took another sip of her drink and shrugged. "Yeah, what about it?"

"How do you think a penanggalan even . . . becomes

a penanggalan?" Alia asked. She hoped her tone was sufficiently casual. The last thing she needed was to go from the New Girl to the Weird Girl Obsessed with Hantu.

Liyana leaned forward, her tone low and conspiratorial. "Only those who know, know," she said. "But my guess is it has to be some really black magic, right? Because it isn't just a thing that happens to you; it's a thing you have to *choose* to become. And it takes somebody reaaaaally evil to want to become . . . that."

Alia gulped. The air in the canteen suddenly felt still, and stale, and suffocating. "Really evil," she echoed.

"Why are you asking, anyway?" Liyana leaned forward, eyebrows raised. "What's the deal?"

"Oh." She couldn't let anyone in. She just couldn't. Not until she figured out how to get rid of it. "Nothing. Just curious."

Liyana sniffed. "Hmm. Well, just be careful what kinds of questions you ask. If all the rumors are true and there really is a penanggalan haunting this town, well . . . you don't want their attention. Trust me."

"I don't," Alia agreed. "I definitely don't." But in her head all she could think was: *What if I already have it?*

13

Really evil.

Really evil.

It takes somebody really evil.

For the rest of the day, the words echoed in her head. If there was even the smallest chance this was true, if Kak Ayu really was a penanggalan . . . she shuddered in the afternoon heat.

But Alia was nothing if not fair and accurate. Sure, Liyana had told her a bunch of things, and she'd sure sounded like she knew what she was talking about. But Liyana also believed that evil monsters could be disguised in grasshopper bodies and shrieked every time one jumped at her; she read about crumpets once in a book and confessed to Alia that she thought they were "cakes shaped like trumpets." She wasn't exactly 100 percent reliable. And Alia wasn't about to get all hysterical and make accusations that ended up being totally wrong. For one, that would be embarrassing. For two, if her sister really was something . . . else . . . then if Alia did try telling her parents and they didn't believe her, all she would have done would be to call attention to herself and let Kak Ayu know that Alia knew her secret. And having Kak Ayu know that, having her realize that Alia was the one person who could jeopardize her cozy little existence in their small town? Well. That had consequences she didn't even want to think about.

She had to be sure.

So when she got home, Alia dropped her things by the door and strode with purpose right up to the one room in the house she was not allowed to enter. Ever.

Mama's study.

Alia had a phone . . . sort of. It had no sim card or data plan, and she was only allowed to use it on the weekends to watch YouTube and play games. Sometimes, she was allowed to take it with her if she went out with her friends and needed a way to stay in contact, which she could only do as long as there was Wi-Fi. Not that this was an issue right now. It's not like she was drowning in social invitations; she barely had any friends, so this was mostly an optimistic fantasy at best. Everything was protected with passwords only Mama knew (Papa was supposed to know them, in theory. But he forgot them regularly). The search engine had so many parental restrictions on it that it was kind of like the digital equivalent of a bank vault. Mama had a lot of Thoughts and Opinions on screen time and the internet and their effects on the minds of young people, and most of them were bad ones.

But Alia needed the internet, and so there was only one thing she could do. She'd have to use Mama's computer.

Sweat dripped from her forehead as she carefully opened the door and stepped inside the study. Her palms felt clammy. All her life, Mama had been known to roar at anyone whose toes crossed the threshold. "My entire life's work is behind that door," she'd say to Alia and Papa. "If either of you does anything that messes it up, *you will feel the consequences.*" But Alia had taken the blame for messing with her things already anyway, hadn't she? She flushed red, still stung with the injustice of it all. *If she thinks I've done it anyway, I might as well do it, and actually get something out of it.*

All over the walls, there were complicated charts and figures; a large standing whiteboard in one corner was full of Mama's scribbles; and one wall was covered in note cards with writing so small and cramped and messy that Alia could barely make anything out.

And sitting on the heavy wooden desk, there it was: the computer.

Alia sat down carefully on the edge of her seat. She'd talked a big game earlier, but it still felt like she should be looking out for booby traps and wiping away her fingerprints so Mama couldn't catch her. Hesitating only slightly, she pressed the power button. Immediately, the screen blinked to life with a merry chime that seemed to echo throughout the room. Alia stopped, heart pumping, hands hovering over the keyboard. *Did anybody hear me?*

It took a second for her to laugh at herself. Nobody was home. Mama had a doctor's appointment, and Kak Ayu was at the mall trying to see if there were any stores hiring.

She turned her attention back to the screen and cracked her knuckles thoughtfully. "All right," she said aloud. "Let's do this."

Mama's home page was the town news portal, and Alia scanned the headlines absentmindedly as she scrolled. Blah blah, politics. Blah blah, the economy. An anime festival happening in the community hall.

A missing kid, only seven years old. In the picture, she wore her dark hair in pigtails. She had a gap-toothed smile and pink ribbons. On her wrist she wore a bracelet of little pink beads. Alia imagined her mother carefully brushing her hair, dividing it into equal parts on each side, and tying the ribbons with a flourish, the way Mama had tied hers when she was little. She would have been around this girl's age the last time they'd lived here.

Seven years old.

Babies, Liyana had said. *And little kids.*

Alia closed her eyes, took a deep breath, and shook her head. *Focus, Alia. One thing at a time.*

Penanggalan, she typed carefully into the search engine. Her eyes widened at the long list of results that popped up. Movies and horror stories, forums filled with hantu hunters and monster enthusiasts, so much horrifically detailed art. She paused on one picture, an illustration where the penanggalan's hair and entrails floated menacingly around its head like massive tentacles, and shuddered.

Is this Kak Ayu? Is this what she is?

Alia was still clicking through website after website when she realized what had been bugging her for the past ten minutes. A faint, insistent noise just on the edge of her hearing, like a mosquito's buzzing, but softer at the edges. She frowned. *What is that?*

She turned her attention back to Wikipedia. But the noise, whatever it was, stayed right there, fading in and out but never going away completely. It was like an itch she couldn't quite reach to scratch. And then, just as she thought it had gone away completely, it wasn't a buzzing anymore.

Out, a voice whispered softly in her ear, soft and low, and Alia yelped.

There was nobody there, nothing but the dust bunnies swaying gently in the darkest corners. Mama didn't enjoy vacuuming, and even though Kak Ayu did the rest of the house now (*perfect, amazing Kak Ayu,* thought Alia sourly), Mama's office was off-limits even to her.

You're imagining it, Alia, she told herself. *Reading all these creepy things is making you jumpy. Get a grip, will you?*

But no sooner did she think this than it happened again. *Out*, something whispered. It was faint and fuzzy, like listening through static. *Get . . . out.*

"Who's there?" Alia called out.

Nobody answered.

Alia waited. In the stillness of the late afternoon, she thought she heard someone—something?—laugh, the sound rustling quietly around her like the wind through the trees.

"That," said Alia aloud, "is quite enough of that." She got up, trying to ignore how hard her knees shook. "I'm going to figure out where it's coming from." *If it's the last thing I do*, her brain added automatically, and she wished immediately that it hadn't.

She cleared the search history—even in the midst of all this, Alia's fear of Mama's wrath held true—and slowly walked out of the room and down the stairs. In scary movies, this would have happened in the pitch black of night, and a floorboard would creak ominously at just the right moment. Alia was almost insulted at how bright and cheery and normal everything around her looked, first in the living room, and then in the kitchen. It made the fear blossoming in her heart make so much less sense. Yet every hair on her body stood on end, and every nerve in her was screaming that something was about to happen, something that she wasn't going to like—

All around her, a ripple suddenly shuddered through the kitchen walls, as if some unknown creature crawled beneath the surface, a creature that was large, a creature that made *clack clack* sounds as it scuttled along, like little claws scraping against wood and concrete.

For a while, there was silence.

Then, from inside the walls, the whispers began again.

Out, they said, soft and wavy as an eel dancing in water. *Get . . . out.* Over and over again. *Out. Out. Out.* And then, louder and more insistent still: *OUT. OUT. OUT.*

Alia covered her ears with both hands, gritting her teeth so hard her jaw ached. *It is too much*, she thought desperately. *It is too much, and I can't bear it.*

Get out, the voices insisted. *Out. Out. GET OUT.*

They were so demanding, so persistent. "Why?" she yelled over the whispers. "Why should I? This is my home!"

GET . . . OUT. GET . . . OUT.

"NO."

Over the chanting, constant and unending, Alia thought she heard another voice, one that whispered right in her ear: *Not you.*

And she opened her mouth, and began to scream.

14

"Alia!"

Alia peeled her eyes open, one after the other. She was on the cold tile of the kitchen floor, and Mama's worried face hovered overhead. "Alia! Are you all right? Talk to me."

Alia swallowed; her mouth felt like someone had rubbed sandpaper all over it. "I—"

"Oh, thank goodness!" Mama flung her arms around Alia so she almost choked. "You're sure you're okay? What happened? Did you faint? Are you sick?"

Alia tried again: "I—" She wished Mama would stop talking for just a minute so she could listen for the whispers.

"Aiya, don't talk too much! You need to rest."

Alia rolled her eyes. "Mama. I'm fine. Really." She struggled to sit up and quickly scanned the walls. But they stayed perfectly still and flat, and not a whisper was heard anywhere.

Mama placed a hand on her forehead, worry written all over her face. "You don't feel warm."

"Because I'm not sick," Alia said irritably. "Really Mama, I'm . . ." she trailed off as her brain caught up with her mouth. *Being sick means staying home, Alia. Alone. While you try and figure out where those voices came from and what they have to do with that monster.* "I mean." She coughed abruptly. "I'm really not feeling that well, now that I think about it."

"Maybe I should call Dr. Yeong." Mama began her looking-for-my-phone dance, patting her pockets, eyes darting left and right. "Where did I put that thing . . . ?"

"I don't think I need a doctor," Alia said, trying her best to appear pale and weak. "I just need some rest. Just staying in bed all day would make me feel a lot better."

"Hmm," Mama said. "Well, if you really aren't well, you'll have to stay home. But you'd be alone, though. I have back-to-back meetings. . . . And Papa's at a conference all day. . . . I could try and cancel my last interview, maybe, and come back early."

"I'll be home."

Alia turned to see Ayu framed in the doorway of the kitchen. She wore a baju kurung covered in tiny flowers in shades of pink and purple, and yet another one of those gauzy white scarves wrapped around her neck. There was nobody she wanted to see less right now than her sister, or as Alia now thought of her, the One Responsible for This Whole Mess. Then she remembered the voices she'd heard. *Get out. Not you.* Then who? Could the house recognize Kak Ayu for what she was? Did it want her gone too?

"Oh, yes!" Mama's face brightened. Alia could practically hear the thought pinging through her head: This is the Perfect Opportunity for My Estranged Daughters to Bond! "Would you mind, Ayu? That would be such a help."

"Not at all." Ayu glanced at Alia and smiled a smile that never quite reached her eyes. "I'd be happy to . . . take care of her."

"Um." It was suddenly hard to breathe. How was she supposed to snoop with Kak Ayu watching her? And was she imagining it, or did the way Kak Ayu said "take care of her" sound . . . sinister? Forget snooping. She didn't think she was even going to be *safe* with her sister around.

"That's wonderful." Mama beamed at her. "Just get

lunch delivered lah if it's too leceh to cook. Something healthy, ya? No fast food. Just . . . attempt something green in there somewhere, please."

"Got it." Ayu grinned at their mother. Had her teeth always gleamed like that in the light? Had they always been that *sharp*? "Don't worry about a thing. I'm sure we'll find ways to keep ourselves occupied."

Mama was smiling at them fondly. "So nice to see you two getting along again," she murmured. Then she tugged at the blouse she wore and sighed. "I'm dying for a shower. The line at the doctor's was *murder*, let me tell you . . ."

Alia coughed. "Mama. I'm actually feeling okay now. Maybe I should go to school tomorrow after all—"

"Nonsense," Mama said briskly as she headed down to her room. "Stay home and rest. Let your sister take care of everything."

"That's right," Ayu said, following behind her. "Let me take care of *everything*."

That's what I'm afraid of, Alia thought desperately.

15

Step two: hands-on research. Aka snooping.

Mama always told Alia that if you fail to plan, you plan to fail. Alia found this comforting. Bad luck meant you *had* to plan; you had to try and anticipate all the ways the universe would let you down. And so that morning, after her parents had kissed her good-bye, she lay in bed and thought about exactly what she needed to do.

Alia's working theory was that Kak Ayu had been responsible for the voices in the walls. She didn't quite know how, but she figured creatures of darkness must have some sorts of powers at their disposal. And really, who else could it have been? And as for why . . . *She's still mad, Alia. You haven't exactly given her the warm, welcoming reception she was probably hoping for. You're screwing up her perfect little family reunion. She had Papa and Mama accusing you of doing stuff before, and now she's found a new way to mess with your head.*

Alia nodded. This was good. This gave her something to work with, something to give shape to the fears that flitted around her brain and help her sort them into neat little boxes. This helped her to *breathe*.

There was a soft *click* and *creak* as the door of her room swung open. "Alia?" Kak Ayu said softly.

Alia stayed as still as she could, eyes closed, breathing deep and even, pretending she was fast asleep. She felt like she might throw up from the stress and the way her heart was racing. Any minute now, she felt like Kak Ayu would snatch back the blanket and point at her and yell "You're faking!"

But instead, she heard the door close and the sound of footsteps heading to the bathroom down the hall. Then the gurgle of the toilet flushing. Then the roar of water.

The shower.

Alia sat bolt upright and threw the covers off. *Now's my chance.*

She crept downstairs softly to where Kak Ayu slept in the living room. On the table sat Kak Ayu's phone. It was an older model, and she didn't bother to password protect it. "What's the point?" She'd shrugged. "I only use it for calls and texts anyway. I have nothing to hide." Just this morning Mama had made her download their usual food delivery app and put Mama's credit card on it. "So you can order lunch," Mama said. "No need to go out."

But that's precisely what Alia needed Ayu to do.

Carefully she opened up the app, then scrolled to payment information.

DELETE.

Are you sure? the app asked her.

Alia paused. Upstairs, she heard the water stop. Quickly, she tapped on *Yes*, tossed the phone back onto the table, and sprinted up the stairs to her room. She'd just managed to get under the covers when Kak Ayu appeared at the door in shorts and a baggy T-shirt, hair still wet, towel wrapped around her neck. "Oh," she said. "You're up. How are you feeling?"

"A little tired," Alia croaked, then tried to keep from shuddering as Ayu pressed a cold hand on her forehead.

"That's weird." Ayu frowned, and Alia felt her heart constrict.

"What?"

"You're so sweaty." Ayu rubbed her hand on her shorts. "Maybe I should take you to the doctor after all."

"Oh, that's not really necessary," Alia said quickly.

"But you know what I'd like, though? What would really make me feel better? Porridge."

"Porridge?"

"Yeah!" Alia nodded enthusiastically. "Especially the bubur ayam from that one restaurant in town. Mak Jah's. You know that one? I really think that would make me feel better."

"Your wish is my command, *master*." There was something softly mocking about the way she said "master," and it made Alia itch. "I'll go put in the order."

Alia smiled as sweetly as she could. "Thanks." Then, as Kak Ayu made her way downstairs, she waited. *Three . . . two . . . one . . .*

"Ugh!"

"What's the matter?" Alia yelled.

There was a clattering up the stairs, then Kak Ayu came into the room, holding her phone and frowning. "There's no credit card info here. I don't know what happened. . . ." She tap-tap-tapped on the screen, as if pressing harder would make the information magically reappear. "I just added it this morning!"

"Oh." Alia let disappointment flood into the one syllable. "And Mama and Papa are both so busy today. There's no way you can call and ask for it either. . . ."

108

"And I don't have my own card yet." Kak Ayu sighed. "I was waiting until I got a real job and a steady paycheck. I don't even have any cash on me right now."

"Oh man." Alia blinked back tears. *That's right, Alia, as heartbroken as you can.* "So I can't have the porridge? I just . . . really wanted it." A single tear slid down her cheek. *That's it, Alia. This is Oscar-worthy stuff.*

Ayu rolled her eyes. "So dramatic for what?" she said. "I'll go into town and get it. I'll drop by an ATM and get some money first. I'll take my bike, so it shouldn't take me long." She sighed as she tied her still-damp hair back with the scrunchie around her wrist. "You should be grateful. I'm only doing this to help Mama and Papa out, you know. After the way you've treated me, the last thing I wanted to do today was be stuck here taking care of you."

Alia snorted. "Yeah, since you disappeared for half my life, I'm pretty sure the least you can do is get me some porridge. Since I'm sick and all. And since Mama probably wouldn't be very happy if she knew you let me *starve* instead of buying me the one thing I was craving."

"Brat." Ayu headed out the door. "Get some rest. I have to go change. Ugh, and it's so hot outside too."

"Our luck sure changed when you came home!" Alia singsonged to her retreating back, but all she got in reply was the irritated click of Ayu's tongue.

She lay back and waited until she heard the key turn in the lock of the front door. Then she stood by the window and watched to make sure Ayu was really, really gone. And only then did she let herself breathe again.

It was time.

Think, Alia. She'd purposely chosen Mak Jah's, which was on the edge of town. It would take Ayu a while to get back. *You have until at least two thirty before she comes home. If you're going to figure out what she's been up to, now's the time to do it.*

Quickly, Alia made her way to the living room—now Ayu's bedroom. It looked the same as it always did, with its two overstuffed sofas covered in hardy, stain-resistant floral patterns, ugly but practical.

Now one of those sofas served as Ayu's bed, and beside it, in the corner, lay a small suitcase, open and filled with neatly folded and arranged clothes, her sister's entire life in one little bag.

Alia knelt down beside this pile of Ayu's worldly possessions and tried to ignore the sharp pang of guilt that blossomed in her belly at the idea of rummaging through another person's things. *You have to do this. You have to figure out what's going on.*

And so she took a deep breath, and began to dive in.

She had no idea what she was looking for, and really, in the beginning, there was nothing to find. There were clothes, and scarves in soft fabrics and softer hues; everything was well taken care of, but you could tell they'd been worn over and over again. There was a pile of books nestled in a corner of the suitcase, many of them religious, some bearing titles about FINDING YOURSELF and LEARNING TO LOVE WHO YOU ARE. Alia had always thought self-help books were kind of corny and embarrassing. "Who buys these things, anyway?" she'd ask, rolling her eyes as they passed those shelves at the bookstore.

Ayu, apparently.

Alia sighed as she put the clothes back where she'd found them. This was hopeless. Nothing here was suspicious; everything bore the signs of a quiet life. Maybe she was imagining it all. Maybe she wasn't finding anything because there was nothing to find. Maybe . . . maybe . . .

Something clinked against her hand.

Maybe she should keep looking.

She pulled out a little drawstring bag. It was full,

and whatever was inside it clicked and clacked against each other as she lifted it out from where it was almost hidden beneath a pile of underwear. She opened it and poured out its contents. It was the most random assortment of things: a gold necklace with a little ice skate pendant. A blue handkerchief with the initials J. S. in one corner. A windup monkey. A pack of tissues printed all over with tiny pandas. A green-and-blue marble. One silver key. All sorts of small knickknacks that didn't seem to have anything to do with each other at all, carried around in this bag the way a small child collects treasures that mean nothing to anyone else.

What did it mean?

Absentmindedly, Alia wound up the monkey and watched as it flipped over and over again on its little clockwork legs. What was Ayu doing with all these things?

The monkey landed on the handkerchief and fell on its side, and Alia went to pick it up and put it away.

And then she froze.

Because the handkerchief had dark brown-red stains seeping through one corner, stains that looked exactly like . . . like . . .

Like blood.

And as she picked it up for a closer look, she saw

it, just hidden beneath a corner of the handkerchief: a bracelet of pink beads. A bracelet far too small for her sister's adult wrist. A bracelet made for a child's wrist; the same bracelet she'd just seen on a little girl with pink ribbons in her pigtails. The phrases flitted through her head. *Missing child. Seven years old. If you see her, please inform the authorities.*

The room began to spin. Alia dropped to her knees, breathing heavily. All around her, just for a moment, the room sighed. *Out*, the voices whispered. *Out*. Only this time, they didn't come from inside the walls. They came from the box in the corner, the box filled with Papa's puppets.

And as Alia watched, the box shuddered.

Not this, she thought, gritting her teeth. *Not now.* She gathered up the things and stuffed them back in the bag with clumsy fingers, being very, very careful not to look at the box in the corner. She tried her best to put it all back exactly as she found it, except for the bracelet. That, she stuffed into her pocket. *I'll think about what to do with it later.*

In the corner, there was a tapping as if someone—something?—was asking to be let in. Or out.

I will not look, Alia told herself. *I will not look.* She began to recite Ayat Kursi under her breath, but fear erased the words from her head and numbed her tongue.

There was a scraping noise, as if something was making its way out of its cardboard confines.

Get . . . out . . .

Alia couldn't help it. She looked.

Papa's prize puppet stood atop the box, propped up against the wall. It was the one he'd received from a mysterious giver, all intricate carvings and carefully-painted leather in black and red and gold and green. As she watched, it raised one arm, as if it was being controlled by invisible hands, and pointed an accusing finger straight at her.

Get . . . out . . .

"Who?" she asked aloud, almost shouting in her fear and anger. "You said not me. So who . . . ?"

"What are you doing down here?" The voice made her yelp, and she whirled around to see Kak Ayu standing in the doorway, staring at her. Behind her, unnoticed, the walls rippled in silent circles, like a whirlpool with Kak Ayu right at its center.

Her, Alia thought, stomach churning. *It's her who needs to get out. The house is rejecting her. It knows she doesn't belong here. It knows she has to go.*

"And who are you talking to? You should be in bed!"

Alia whirled around. The puppet was gone. The box was shut. It was as if nothing had happened at all.

"Oh." Alia paused, striving for a casual tone. "I just came down to . . . get a drink." The bracelet in her pocket felt like it weighed ten tons. *Don't look at the suitcase, Alia. Don't look at the wall. Don't look at the box. Don't look at your pocket. You just came down for a glass of water, remember? Nothing more than that.*

Kak Ayu held up a pink plastic bag. "I got your porridge." She frowned and glanced behind her. "What are you looking at?" But the wall behind her was smooth and still.

"Oh! Awesome! Thank you so much!" Alia said, her voice strangled. "That was so nice of you!"

"Yeah, well." Kak Ayu set the bag down on the coffee table, looking at Alia strangely. "That's . . . an enthusiastic response. Do you want to eat?"

"Um. Maybe later? I'm not that hungry right now." She glanced quickly at the open suitcase. Was everything back where it was supposed to be? Had Kak Ayu noticed?

It was only a second, but when she looked up again, she realized Kak Ayu was just standing there, watching her. Her eyes flicked over to her suitcase.

Alia gulped. "Anyway! I'm just going to . . . uh . . . get a little more rest. Feeling a little lightheaded right now, you know how it is. I'll eat later. Thanks again for the food!" Then she ran up the stairs, two at a time, almost tripping on the second to last step, and threw herself into her room, locking the door quietly behind her and then leaning on it to take a breath.

Get out, the puppet had whispered. *Not you*, the voices in the walls had told her.

But how? How was she supposed to get rid of this monster?

Whoosh.

Alia's heart almost stopped, hearing the sound at the window. Surely she'd been through enough today?

Whoosh.

Alia closed her eyes. She knew she was supposed to be brave, to gather evidence. But she just didn't think her heart could take it right now, not after what had just happened.

There was another *whoosh*. Then, almost immediately after, a quiet rattling sound against the windowpane. Then a soft rubbing sound, like something moving gently, slowly over smooth wood. A hand, perhaps. Or . . . an entrail gliding across the sill, looking for the latch to swing the window wide open . . .

Alia thought she might actually pee her pants.

For a moment, everything was still. Then, suddenly—

BANG.

Whatever hit the window did it so hard, it seemed to Alia that the walls shook.

Alia choked back a scream. Then she bolted to the window.

But there was nothing there, nothing but clouds dotting the bright blue afternoon sky.

17

Step three: lay your trap.

"Five . . . six . . . seven . . ." Alia counted softly as she placed the last nail down and stepped back to survey her work.

She'd had to wait until her parents got home, then been forced to sit as still as she could and pretend to eat at dinner, making polite small talk until they'd finally headed to bed, and then she'd had to wait until they'd finally fallen asleep in their room, and the creature that was her sister was asleep on the sofa. But once the house was silent, she'd locked up every door and window as quickly and quietly as she could. Each now boasted a neat row in front of it, made up of every sharp object she could find in the house, including all the nails in her father's toolbox, screws that she'd carefully removed from objects that she felt sure didn't really need them, like remote controls and chairs—only one or two, of course, Alia wasn't *that* silly—and all the thumbtacks from the bulletin board that held the note cards Mama used to plan her book chapters. These were now arranged in a neat little pile on her desk. Mama would be furious, but she would thank Alia when it turned out that she was preventing Ayu from . . . from . . .

It was at this point that Alia's thoughts always screeched to a hard stop. Every once in a while as she worked, she reached into her pocket to caress the pink beads nestled there. A little girl missing, possibly dead; and her sister to blame for it all. *How could she?* Alia thought, blinking back the sharp sting of tears. *How could she do it?*

The instructions she'd found on the internet—before the walls had started whispering to her, anyway—had been clear. It was a passage from an old book, one called *Hikayat Abdullah*. It said you could trap a penanggalan by laying mengkuang outside your doors and windows, so the bits of entrails that hung from its head would get caught and it wouldn't be able to fly away.

Alia had no mengkuang—but she had nails. And it

stood to reason that one sharp object was as good as any other, right?

She hoped so, anyway. Because it was well and good doing this to keep penanggalans from coming inside, but nobody seemed to have any instructions for what to do when the creature was right there in the house with you, and could creep up on you *at any minute*.

(The book also said you could kill a penanggalan by filling its neck hole with nails. Or Alia figured you could stab the body and be done with it. Logically, she was aware this would make sense—that you would get rid of the problem entirely all at once. But she couldn't quite bring herself to think about actually doing it. She just wanted to trap the thing to stop it from hurting any more people; she figured the job of what to do with it once it was trapped rested entirely on her parents. *Sometimes*, Alia thought to herself, *you just need grown-ups to help make the tough calls, and this was one of those times*.)

Carefully, she stepped over the final row of nails in front of their front door, closed it gently behind her—quietly, so as not to wake up the creature that slumbered on the living room sofa. *There. Now everything is going to be—*

"ADOIIIIIIIIIIIIII!" The scream ripped through the stillness of the night like a knife. Alia ran toward the sound, bounding up the stairs two at a time, her heart racing. Had it worked? Had she trapped herself a penanggalan? Would she finally have the proof she needed to tell her parents exactly what was going on?

In front of Mama and Papa's bedroom door, Kak Ayu sat in a crumpled heap, groaning and rubbing her foot. Alia skidded to a stop and stared at her. The creature's head seemed to be quite firmly in place, but it couldn't hurt to try and get closer and see if she'd managed to snare any loose entrails or something. . . .

"What," Kak Ayu said through gritted teeth, "is going *on* here?"

Alia's shoulders sagged. "Oh. You're okay."

"Of course I'm not okay!" Kak Ayu shrieked. "I stepped on a thumbtack! Almost an entire row of thumbtacks! I could need a tetanus shot or something!"

Alia couldn't help snorting at this, remembering what she'd read online: *The first penanggalan was a woman. She used the magic arts of a devil in whom she believed, and she devoted herself to his service night and day until she was able to fly.* Somehow she doubted someone who'd made a deal with the devil was going to suffer much from tetanus.

"You're fine," Alia said. It was hard to keep the disappointment out of her voice.

Kak Ayu's eyes narrowed as she slowly got to her feet. "And just what exactly were you trying to achieve here?"

Alia's pulse quickened beneath her sister's gaze. "I . . . don't know what you mean."

"Don't give me that." She leaned forward, so close their noses almost touched. For a second, Alia forgot to breathe. "I *know* you know."

Just then the door flew open and Papa lumbered up, sleep-rumpled and narrow-eyed. "What's the matter?" he said grumpily.

Alia opened her mouth to speak . . .

. . . then watched as Kak Ayu swiftly stepped forward and in one smooth motion swept the row of thumbtacks aside with the side of her foot so that Papa wouldn't notice. "Nothing, Papa," she said sweetly. "Alia and I were just thinking of getting ourselves a little midnight snack. Right, Alia?"

Alia didn't want to think about what kinds of snacks a penanggalan would be looking for at midnight. "Right," she managed to choke out.

Papa's eyes narrowed as he surveyed first one, then the other. "Don't eat nonsense," he finally grunted, adjusting the sarong that was threatening to come loose at any moment. "It's too late for that. And Alia, you should be in bed. Got school tomorrow."

"Okay, Papa," Alia said meekly.

"Good night, Papa," Kak Ayu said, and she lifted herself up on the tips of her toes to plant a gentle kiss on Papa's cheek. This earned her a small smile, and Alia almost wanted to cry at the softness she saw in his eyes. *I can't let you do this to them.* She glowered at Ayu. *I can't let you hurt them. Not their bodies, and not their hearts either.*

The door shut with a firm *click.*

Alia turned to see Kak Ayu staring directly at her, arms folded, one eyebrow raised. "You're wasting your time. I don't know what exactly you're trying to do here, but I'm not out to hurt you, okay, Alia? I just want to rebuild my life. Be part of a family again." She bit her lip. "You don't have to want to be my sister, not right away. But could you give me a chance to prove myself, at least?"

Alia thought about all she'd read and learned. *Really evil. Devil. Blood. Missing child.* She crossed her arms, trying her best to be brave. "No."

Kak Ayu just stared at her for a minute. Then she nodded. "Fine. If we can't be sisters, or even friends, then let's just stay out of each other's way." She turned and walked softly back down the stairs. But Alia thought she heard her say as she left, just within earshot: "Because trust me. You don't want me as an enemy."

She knows, Alia thought. *She knows I know what she is.* And even though the night was sweltering hot, she shivered.

18

"Could you stop?" Charlene hissed at Alia in the middle of history class. "You've kicked me in the shin twice now. Cut it out."

"Sorry, sorry." It wasn't Alia's fault. Swinging her legs just helped her think better. Alia had spent all morning going over the events of last night. Each time, she got more and more annoyed with herself. She'd done the worst thing she could possibly do: underestimate her enemy. And now the monster knew she was after it.

It's only a matter of time, she thought darkly, *before it begins fighting back.*

The only solution was to act before it had the chance. She had to get proof—real, solid proof that Mama and Papa couldn't possibly ignore—that Kak Ayu wasn't who she said she was. That she was a danger to them all. That she was the penanggalan.

"Ow!"

"Sorry, Charlene, sorry."

Alia bent low over her desk, as if she too was working on her history notes, and began to make plans instead.

She concentrated so hard, it took a while to realize that something was wrong. But it was when she paused for a sip of water from her bottle that she heard it. The usual *scritch scritch scritch* of pencil on paper from Charlene's desk had been replaced instead by slow, rhythmic, long scratches instead.

Which was weird. They were meant to be writing notes, not drawing pictures.

Alia frowned and glanced over at her friend. "Char? What are you—"

But she never managed to finish her sentence. Charlene was staring down at her book. On the page, her usually neat handwriting grew progressively messier and more unreadable, until it faded into nothing but a long line going from one end of the page to the other. It was this line that Charlene was tracing, over and over again, so much that the pencil had torn right through the page.

And still she kept going. Long, slow scratches, over and over.

"Charlene?" Alia gulped hard. She reached out a trembling hand to rest on her friend's arm. "Are you okay?"

Charlene froze.

Then slowly, she turned her head to look at Alia. Her eyes had a strange glint in them that Alia had never seen before.

Charlene smiled, a slow, wide smile that bared all her teeth. "Don't worry, Alia," she whispered. "They believe in me, see? And now they'll believe in you too." Then, as suddenly as it had begun, it was over. Charlene glanced down at her book and gasped. "Oh! Oh no! What did I do?"

Alia blinked. "Um. I . . . I don't . . ." She peered closely at her friend. "Are you . . . okay? You don't remember what just happened?"

"I ruined it!" Charlene was totally focused on her notes as she sighed and reached for her eraser. "I must've dozed off or something. Ugh, the teacher's gonna kill me, I swear." And though she kept talking as she did her best to fix her work, Alia was no longer listening.

What had just happened?

Alia didn't know how not to be scared. But she did know how to be persistent. She had to. When you were as unlucky as she was, it was either you kept trying or you never got anything done.

The incident with Charlene, whatever it was, had something to do with her sister. She was sure of it. It was all connected: this, and the whispers in the walls, and the puppet. The weirdness only began once her sister reappeared. It had to be her who was the source of all this. How could it not be?

The real issue with her plan, she decided, was that she'd gotten ahead of herself—and no, she hadn't made that pun on purpose. She'd tried to go straight to setting traps when what she really needed was backup. She needed her parents on her side, so that they could be the ones to figure out the tough stuff, not her. Because yes, Alia had read a lot of books and watched a lot of movies where kids got to be the heroes, but nine times out of ten she'd wondered why, when getting parents involved would have made life easier for *everyone*.

Alia sighed. Stories were stories, but this was real life, and when you fail to plan *correctly*, you plan to fail.

And so, Alia had to face it. She needed a new plan: *Step three (revised): bring in the big guns.*

For the next couple of nights, she snuck out of her

room when her parents were asleep, sat at the top of the stairs, and waited, phone in hand, for some sign that the creature who lived downstairs was going to reveal itself. She was going to catch this on video, no matter what. And then there was no way her parents could deny what was happening.

And, just as if Kak Ayu knew exactly what she was doing . . . nothing happened.

Of course she knows, Alia thought bitterly. *Of course. She's always one step ahead. Always watching me.* It almost made her want to give up.

But then, one night, when Papa was away on a field trip and Mama was up late working in her study, Alia fell asleep without meaning to, right there at the top of the stairs. And when she woke up, it wasn't to whispers in the walls, but to music blaring throughout the house, so loud it shook the floorboards.

She rubbed the sleep out of her eyes and frowned. "What in the world . . . ?"

The music stopped.

In the silence, Alia's heartbeat felt incredibly loud. She had no idea where Mama was. Or Kak Ayu. *Her head might not be here, then,* she thought, and she was about to head down the stairs to the living room to take a picture when the music blared through the house once more. *I WANT TO BREAK FREE. I WANT TO BREAK FREE.*

It was coming from Mama's office, on the third floor, right above her head. Alia took to the stairs, two at a time, gritting her teeth as she went. The music felt like it was rattling her brain.

The door to Mama's office was open. Alia peeked inside. "Mama?" she called.

Click. The music stopped.

Mama was standing with her back to the door, facing her CD player, dressed in one of her bedtime batik caftans. Her hair hung, curly and wild, down to her shoulders. In her hand she clutched a CD case that Alia recognized. *The Best of Queen.* In a world of Spotify and streaming, Mama still stuck firmly to her CDs. She kept them alphabetically arranged in neat rows on the shelf below her player, and this particular album was one of her favorites.

Click. *OH, I WANT TO BE FREE, BABY. OH, HOW I WANT TO BE FREE.*

"Mama?" Alia had to yell to be heard over the wails of the electric guitar. "What are you doing?"

Mama said nothing. She didn't even move, except to push the button on the CD player.

Click. Silence.

Click. GOD KNOWS I WANT TO BREAK FREE.

"MAMA." Panic turned Alia's cries into an almighty yell. "STOP!" She ran into the room and tugged at her mother's arm.

Mama whirled around to face her, and Alia stepped back without even meaning to. Because there was something about her face that made Alia's stomach clench. Just like Charlene, Mama's smile stretched wide, showing all her teeth. And just like Charlene, the smile never reached her eyes, which themselves just stared at Alia, so blank they might as well have been buttons.

Click. Silence.

"Hello, sayang," Mama said quietly.

Alia recoiled. It was Mama's mouth that moved, and Mama's face that stared at her. But the voice that came out of her wasn't hers.

It was the same as the voices in the walls. The voice of the puppet as it stared at Alia with its painted eyes.

"Mama." Alia swallowed. "What . . . what are you doing?"

Mama's hand hovered uncertainly over the CD player's play button. And as Alia watched, her brows began to furrow. Sweat beaded on her forehead. "I don't know," she hissed through her teeth. "I don't know." Her fingers shook.

Suddenly her hand flew toward the button as if something had let it loose. She hit play and then mashed her finger on the volume button, so that it went all the way up. *I WANT, I WANT, I WANT TO BREAK FREE*, Freddie Mercury bellowed.

"Mama, stop, stop, please, Mama," Alia yelled. It felt like every bone in her body hurt. She fell to the floor and curled up, closing her eyes tight, covering her ears. "Please, Mama, please," she said, over and over, until gentle hands prized her own away.

"Alia?" Mama whispered.

Alia looked at her. The music had stopped, and Mama's eyes and voice were her own again.

"Mama!" She collapsed in a grateful heap into her mother's arms, and Mama clung to her like a life raft. "What happened to you? It's like you weren't *there*."

Mama's hands were damp with sweat. "I don't know what happened," she said, her voice shaking. Alia could feel Mama's tears soaking her hair. "I don't know. I don't know. I know you're scared. I am too, sayang. I'm so sorry I did that to you. I'm so sorry."

"I'm sorry too," Alia whispered. And she was. She

was sorry that she hadn't done something sooner. Sorry that she hadn't been quick enough to spare her mother. Sorry that she'd taken this long to get the monster out of their house, and out of their lives.

But the anger was back now, burning brighter than her fear. And now the only thing that was going to be sorry was Kak Ayu.

19

Alia awoke hopeful for the first time in what felt like forever. Sure, Mama would be a complete wreck this morning. But now she had experienced it too. Mama *had* to believe her. Alia hummed as she got ready. It's not like she wanted Mama to be completely traumatized. It was just that she was sure she'd be able to talk to her mother now, convince her that Ayu was the reason all these things were happening, that the house was using any means necessary to tell them to get her out. Hadn't the song Mama played spelled it out for them? *I WANT TO BREAK FREE.* It was trapped in this nightmare, just as they were.

"I do too," Alia told the house, patting the wall beside her bed. "I do too."

So she was utterly unprepared to head down to breakfast and see her mother smiling as she doled pancakes out onto plates. "Good morning, sayang!" Mama sang out.

"Good . . . morning." Alia slid into her seat and stared at her mother. "Are you . . ." She glanced around quickly to see if anyone was listening. "Are you okay?" she asked softly.

"Me? I'm fine! Why would you—" A look of realization dawned on Mama's face, and she laughed. "Oh, you mean that episode last night! I was so tired, I must have been sleepwalking. All those deadlines, the stress . . . you know how it is." She squeezed Alia's shoulder gently. "Sorry if I scared you, sayang."

Alia blinked back tears. All the hope she'd carried down the stairs with her evaporated into nothing in the morning sunlight. "But Mama. You were *possessed*."

"Oh, baby." Mama reached out to give her a quick hug. "Sleepwalking can be such a terrifying thing. I'm sorry you had to see that. I'll go to the doctor and see if he can sort me out, okay?"

The lump in Alia's throat was too big for any pancake to get past. She stood up hurriedly, pushing her chair back so fast, it almost tipped over. "Excuse me," she mumbled. "I'm going to go . . . get ready for school."

"But Alia," her mother called after her. "What about breakfast?"

Alia didn't answer. As she passed the living room, she thought she heard a sigh from the corner where the puppet box stood, a long, weary sigh, heavy with disappointment.

Me too, house, she thought bitterly. *Me too.*

So it was back to square one.

Alia ignored her own exhaustion and went back to her vigil at the top of the stairs, night after night after night. And though she had yet to see Kak Ayu take flight, she was still learning the ways of her enemy. She learned that it took Kak Ayu ages to fall asleep, and when she did, she tossed and turned and called out in her sleep. Alia knew this because she'd startled awake the first time she heard Ayu's voice floating through the darkness. "Please. *Please.*" There was so much desperation in her voice; so much sadness. She wondered what it was the monster was begging for, until she heard Kak Ayu finally get up at the first strains of the call to prayer. That was when Alia found out that Ayu wept as she prayed each dawn. "Please," she heard Ayu's voice whisper, "please help me stop. Please make me good."

And *that* was how Alia learned that no matter how else she felt, she still hated to see her sister cry.

She's a monster, Alia reminded herself. *Nothing more*. But it was hard to see that tear-stained face and stop her heart from feeling an echo of the same ache.

Tonight was quiet so far; she could hear the rustle of bedding as Ayu moved restlessly on the sofa, but nothing else. Alia was just rubbing her tired eyes and wondering if it mattered if she just took a little nap when . . . when . . .

There was a sound. A sound she recognized.

Alia's eyes flew open. It wasn't the hum of the ceiling fan, or Kak Ayu mumbling nonsense in her sleep. It wasn't the creak of a step outside as Mama went downstairs for a drink, or Papa's snores reverberating from their bedroom like a chainsaw.

Squelch. Squelch. Squelch.

It was *her*.

Alia crept as quietly as she could down the stairs, phone in hand—she'd worn socks specially, even though they made her feet sweat. At the bottom she paused, listening intently. The squelching stopped, and there was silence.

What was the creature doing?

Alia chewed nervously on her bottom lip. Sure, every inch of her wanted to turn around and run away as fast as she could. But logically, her brain was telling her: You need to get closer. You need to capture this on video. You need to do this, for Mama and Papa.

Fine, brain. You win. Alia dropped down and began to crawl. The bottom of the stairs faced the front door; to her left was the living room. One of the sofas stood right near the entrance; the other, across the room, beneath a row of tall bay windows. That was the one Ayu slept on. Alia crawled quickly over behind the first sofa, then paused. Her heart was pounding so loudly, she was sure the monster could hear her. Carefully, she craned her neck to peek around the corner, phone at the ready . . .

. . . and nearly screamed. The moonlight cast sharp shadows on the wall, and Alia saw the shape of a head, a head with long dark hair and no body. Long, thick shapes trailed and dangled from its neck like tentacles. Heart pounding, eyes blurry with tears, Alia watched as the shadow hung, suspended for a moment, before she heard a *whoosh*—a familiar *whoosh*, she realized with a shock, a *whoosh* she knew well—followed by a rustle of curtains.

The room was still, and Alia steadied herself to take a proper look at last.

On the sofa where her sister slept was a body, still arranged in peaceful slumber, a body that ended at the neck, still leaning against the pillow, with a gentle dent where a head ought to be.

Alia gulped, hard. The hand holding the phone shook, but she still held tight, letting the camera linger on the . . . thing . . . on the sofa. Then, quickly, she padded to the window.

And there she was.

Ayu was in the air, entrails dangling from her neck as she soared into the sky. And as Alia watched, she tried her best to sort through the messy tangle of feelings that lodged itself in her chest and made it hard to breathe—disgust, and fear, and as she caught a glimpse of the look on Ayu's face as she leaned into the breeze, a strange sense of envy. Because Ayu looked happy.

She looked free.

Alia shook her head. "Pull yourself together, woman," she scolded herself. "Pay attention and focus. Remember everything she's done. The spying and the missing girl, the voices in the walls, the way Charlene and Mama were possessed. *Remember.*" And she zoomed in until there could be no mistaking who it was, zoomed in so her parents couldn't deny the truth any longer, zoomed in just enough to see Ayu freewheeling through the stars, moving to music only she could hear.

20

"Is there a reason you had to wake us up like this?" Mama grumbled as she sat up. Beside her, Papa sighed a deep, weary sigh, his eyes still closed.

"Must this happen every other night? Are your children acting up again?"

"They're your children too!"

"Not at—" Papa paused to peel open one eye and check the time on his phone, and groaned. "Yarabi! Not at 12:47 a.m., they're not. What's going on, Alia?"

"It had to be now," Alia explained. "Because she's gone now. Look at this," she said, shoving her phone in Mama's face. Her hands were still sweaty and the phone almost slipped from her grasp; she caught it just before it smashed face-first against the wooden floor.

"What am I looking at?" Mama squinted at the

141

screen, still bleary-eyed. "Where are my reading glasses? Abang, do you know where I put them?"

There was only a mumbled reply from beneath the covers.

"This is serious, Ma!" Alia thought she might cry.

"All right, all right, sabar." Mama finally found her glasses on her bedside table and placed them on her nose. "Yes, yes, okay, show me."

Alia handed her phone over. "Just press play."

"Fine."

Alia waited with bated breath as her mother peered at the screen. Mama stayed silent for a long time. Then she nudged Papa, who grunted.

"No," Mama said, and was it Alia's imagination, or had her voice changed? "You want to see this."

Papa sighed and sat up. "What now—" he began before Mama quietly showed him the video.

Alia couldn't bear it anymore. "She's a penanggalan!" The words ripped themselves from her tongue, loud and impossible to take back. "Don't you see? She can take her head off and fly around! She's doing it *right now*! And she's *hurting people*."

Alia didn't know what she expected. Tears, maybe, or loud protest, or even laughing disbelief. It wasn't this heavy, weighted silence, or the way they looked at her, and then each other, wide-eyed and stricken, but completely, totally unsurprised.

They knew. They had known all along.

"How could you?" she spit out. "How *could* you?"

Mama shifted uncomfortably. "We just thought . . . We wanted . . . We were trying to find the right way to . . ."

"To tell me my sister is a *monster*?"

Mama flinched. "Alia . . ."

"Didn't you think that maybe it would be important to mention it to me?" Alia said. Her voice was getting louder and louder, but she didn't care. "Didn't you think that maybe it would be, oh, just a liiiiittle bit unsafe to have a *creature* like this in our house?"

"Alia," Papa said warningly. "Don't call your sister that."

"Don't call THAT my SISTER."

Mama reached out a hand for hers, but Alia snatched it back. Betrayal surged through her veins, red-hot and restless. "We were trying to protect both of you," Mama said quietly. "You, and Ayu too. Figure out the best way to do all of this. Goodness knows it's been a challenge for us too, accepting this knowledge. But

Ayu is family, and your family are the ones that should never turn their backs on you. No matter what."

Alia felt tears sting her eyes. "But turning toward someone shouldn't mean you turn away from someone else. And you're turning your back on me right now. You, of all people! You've been possessed, for crying out loud! This house wants her out, and *so do I*! And you're not listening to me!"

Mama sighed. "I am, sayang. I'm right here, and I'm listening. I'm just not sure what it is you're trying to say. . . ."

"Yeah, Alia." Kak Ayu stood in their parents' doorway, her arms folded, hurt etched into every line on her face. "What are you trying to say?"

Alia ignored her. "I'm saying she's dangerous!" she told her parents.

"I am not!"

Alia whirled around. "You've been spying on us! Admit it! You have no problem hurting other people to get what you want. And the missing kid?"

"What?!" Kak Ayu stared at her, both angry and bewildered. "What are you *talking* about? You're the one snooping through my things, acting like I'm the one not to be trusted even though I haven't *done anything wrong*—"

"Except sell your soul to become a penanggalan! Even our *house* doesn't want you!"

"Our house? What are you even talking ab—"

"GIRLS," Papa bellowed. "Can you please. Be. Quiet."

Alia clamped her mouth shut. She knew if she spoke even a single word more that she'd burst into tears. Behind her, Kak Ayu subsided too, though her face was dark as an impending storm, as if she had much more that she wanted to say.

"Now." Papa smoothed back his rumpled hair. "We made the decision to welcome Ayu back into this family. In hindsight, this was not something we should have done without letting Alia know the full story." He leaned over and placed a gentle hand on Alia's shoulder. "We are sorry. Very sorry. This was disruptive enough for you without . . . everything else on top of it. We did what we thought was best, but now we know it wasn't best at all."

Alia felt her lips tremble. "She's going to hurt people, Mama," Alia whispered, sweeping the back of her hand roughly across her eyes so nobody would see her tears. "She already has. See?" She took her phone, swiped quickly over to the screenshots of the article she'd saved, and shoved it back into Mama's hand. *Please let them see. Please let them understand.*

Mama scanned the text quickly. "So?" she asked. "What am I looking at here?"

"So?" Alia jabbed at the screen. "Look at her wrist! And look at this!" She drew the pink beads from her pocket with a flourish. "It's the *same bracelet*. I found it in Kak Ayu's things."

"Sayang." Mama looked at Alia sternly. "Why were you looking through your sister's personal belongings, hmm?"

"That's not important right now!" Alia couldn't believe her ears. "Did you hear anything I just said? We have to stop her before she hurts more people! We have to—"

Mama reached out a hand to smooth away the baby hairs that stuck to Alia's sweaty forehead. "Alia, sayang. What reason do you have to believe Ayu is going to hurt anyone?"

"I just know it." Alia sniffed. "It's in her nature. She can't help herself."

"She hasn't hurt anyone since she's been here, has she?"

"That we know of for sure." It was getting hard to tamp down her frustration. "And why do we want to hang around waiting until she does, anyway? Do we have to wait for bodies to start turning up before you'll believe me?"

"I'm not going to do anything," Kak Ayu said, her voice low.

Mama spoke carefully, as though she were trying to choose the very best words. "We know there's been a lot to get used to," she said. "But it would help if you both tried to accept each other. No tricks—" She darted a glance at Kak Ayu, shaking her head when it seemed like a protest was about to be launched. "And no snooping through personal belongings." This part was directed at Alia.

Papa sighed. "Alia. Please, listen to me. You are our daughter, and so is Ayu, and we love you both. We can't say we've ever dealt with a situation like this before, but we're doing our best. We're just asking for you to do the same. All right?"

Frustration clawed at Alia's throat so that it made her want to scream. "Fine," she finally managed. "Fine. All right. I'll go back to bed now." She stomped out of the room, giving her sister a wide berth. Sleep was going to be impossible, but if she stayed in the same room as the monster for one more minute, she thought she might scream.

Only when she pushed the door open, she was met by the sight of the walls bubbling as if pimples bloomed across their painted beige faces.

"What in the world?"

She bent down for a closer look. Each pimple was about the size of her fist, and now that she was closer she realized that they were pulsating gently. As if they were breathing.

As if they were alive.

The idea made her recoil in horror, and she scurried backward, accidentally bumping into one of the pustules with her shoulder . . .

. . . which caused it to burst, covering one side of her with a gray-green ooze that smelled of rotten eggs.

Alia gagged. "MAMA!" she yelled, trying her best not to breathe, or think about how the slime dripping down her torso looked like snot, or if it did, then what kind of creature had produced it. "PAPA! HELP!"

There was the thunderous sound of her entire family racing down the hallway. "APA DIA? WHAT IS IT? WH—" Mama was the first to arrive. The sight of Alia and her walls made her stop dead in her tracks. She clamped a hand to her mouth. "Ya Allah. What . . . How . . ."

Behind her, Papa skidded to a stop, nearly crashing into a wall. "What is it, what's going . . . WHAT IS THAT?"

"It's the house!" Alia sobbed, pointing a finger straight at Kak Ayu, who shrank back, a shocked look on her face. "It wants her gone! She's the reason for all of this!"

"It's not," Ayu whispered. "It's not me."

At the sound of her voice, the wall pimples began to pulse even faster. And this time, when the voices came, they weren't whispers anymore. They were louder and clearer with every moment that passed. *Get us out. Get us out. Get us out, Alia, get us out.*

Alia stared at her sister, stricken. *It's not her they're talking about. It's something else. Something that wants to get out. That wants to break free . . .*

"Girls." Mama was pale. "Get behind me. And start reciting Ayat Kursi. Now." Her lips began to move swiftly as she recited the familiar lines, and Alia and Ayu followed suit, though Alia was so scared, she barely remembered what she was supposed to say.

The pimples began to move so fast, it was as if they were vibrating.

Get us out, the voices growled and shrieked and moaned. *Get us out. GET US OUT.*

And then there was a sudden roar, and a chorus of panicked screaming as the lights flickered on and off and on again, and a pop and a squelch as every single pimple burst, all at the same time.

Then nothing more.

21

They sat around the dining table, the four of them. They made an incongruous-looking group, Alia thought. There was Mama in her batik caftan in shades of hot pink and orange, feet jammed into worn house slippers; there was Abah in pelikat pants and a white Pagoda-brand T-shirt with a constellation of little holes blooming near the neck; there was Alia in her oversize Garfield T-shirt and black sweatpants with a hole in the knee; and there was Kak Ayu in her silky, stripy blue pajamas buttoned all the way to the top, her hand fiddling restlessly with her neck.

For some reason, Mama had decided to pull out the leftovers from dinner, even though it was two o'clock in the morning. "Everything is easier on a full stomach," she said.

Alia wasn't sure anything could make this easier.

She'd tried to clean as much of the goo off herself as she could, but she could still feel it on her skin and smell it in the air. The sight of the food just made her want to throw up.

Across the table, Kak Ayu sat quietly, staring at her hands. She didn't look anybody in the eye.

"Now," their mother said crisply, and they both jumped. "Girls. Do you have any idea what's going on?" Her words were addressed to both of them, but her eyes were on Kak Ayu's face, and in them Alia saw so many things: anger and hurt and pain and a desperate plea, one that said, *Please, let this not have been you. Please let our faith in you have paid off.*

"I don't know, Mama," Kak Ayu said quietly, and Alia mumbled her agreement. She could feel a knot growing in the pit of her stomach, the kind of knot that used to grow there when Mama and Papa and Kak Ayu got in their fights with the screaming and the yelling and the banging of doors.

"Are you sure?" Papa said. He was trying so hard to be gentle; Alia could tell.

Kak Ayu's lips trembled, but her gaze never faltered. "I didn't do anything," she said, looking first at one parent, then the other. "Don't you trust me?"

Mama sighed as she ran a hand through her

disheveled hair. She was wearing her favorite caftan, the one with the rip from armpit to waist that she just said made it "even more airy," and somehow this made Alia feel guilty even though she hadn't done anything. *Mama shouldn't have to deal with this. Mama should be relaxing in the living room with her feet up, in her airy caftan, watching* Gegar Vaganza *or something instead of dealing with this mess.*

Once again she felt that flame flare up inside her, that twinge of anger and resentment toward her sister and all the baggage she'd weighed them down with as soon as she'd walked back through their door. "Why couldn't you just have left us alone?" she muttered. She couldn't help herself.

"Alia. That's enough." Mama turned back to Kak Ayu, whose head had somehow sunk even lower. "I don't want to *not* trust you," she said quietly.

"Then say you believe me." Kak Ayu's lips trembled. "Say you believe I had nothing to do with this. *Say it.*"

"Ayu," Papa said gently. "We just want to be sure."

Kak Ayu stared at both of them, and the pain in her eyes was so clear that Alia had to look away. "Fine," she said quietly. "Here. Is this enough?" And she slid her phone across the table toward their parents.

Alia peered over her mother's shoulder. It was a news article, dated three days ago. There was a Facebook post embedded in the text:

We are so thankful that our little girl was found safe and sound, and we wanted to express our gratitude to every Malaysian who shared her pic, prayed for us, sent out search parties, watched over our family. Bless you all. No one takes care of each other like Malaysians do. We are truly ONE FAMILY!!!!

There was a string of emojis, and a photo attached.

There she was: that gap-toothed smile; shirt slightly grubbier than before; pigtails still in place, though strands of hair had managed to escape and the pink ribbons were gone—and no pink bracelet on her wrist.

The missing girl had been found. And Alia had been . . . wrong.

Guilt made her blood burn in her veins. *Say something, Alia. You have to say something.* But before she could open her mouth, the lights flickered.

The four of them stared at each other, stricken. "It could just be a coincidence," Papa said, and Alia could tell he was striving for a light, jovial tone. "Hell of a time for the electricity to fail, eh? Just—"

"Just bad luck," Alia whispered through dry lips.

Suddenly a gale began to whip around the room,

a howling, shrieking force that drove them to their knees and made talking impossible. "HANG ON!" Papa yelled, and Alia grit her teeth and clutched at the wooden legs of the dining room table. *Don't let go, Alia*, she thought to herself desperately, digging her knees into the ground and willing herself not to move. *Whatever you do, don't let go.*

The wind swirled on and on, making their eyes water. From above, there was the tinkling crash of breaking glass, and then another, and then another, as one by one, every lightbulb in the house burst. "Watch out!" Mama shrieked, and Alia crouched even lower, heart pounding like thunder in her chest, using her free arm to shield her head and trying not to scream as shards and splinters of glass came tumbling down around her like snowflakes. And finally, the gale slowed down to a gentle breeze that wafted from spot to spot in the room, seeming for all the world as if it was skipping playfully along.

"Is everyone all right?" Mama asked urgently. "Alia, are you hu—" She stopped and sucked a breath in through her teeth. Alia followed the direction of her gaze and saw her father trying quickly to wipe away the blood that dripped slowly down from a long, thin scratch at his temple.

"It's nothing," he said quickly. "Just a nick. It doesn't hurt." He sat back at the table and grabbed a tissue from the box. Bright red blossomed into the soft white fibers as he dabbed at his face.

Alia whipped her head around to stare into her mother's stricken eyes. Then they both turned to Ayu, whose face was pale, and whose eyes were focused on that trail of blood.

"Kak Ayu," Alia whispered. "Don't."

Ayu glanced at her for only a second, but in that moment Alia could see the same desire she'd seen when she'd cut her finger, the same thirst that had scared her so badly. But this time she looked, really looked, and she saw so much more: rage, and determination, and above all, love.

And suddenly, she understood.

Kak Ayu closed her eyes and took a deep, shaky breath. "I'm okay," she said softly, then shook herself, setting her chin. "I'm okay," she said, louder this time, certainty threaded through the words like steel.

In the dark room, something cackled, low and soft at first, and then getting louder and more out of control, as if someone had heard the funniest joke in the world.

"'Okay,' she says!" a voice said merrily. "'Okay'!

Look around you, my girl, and see the damage you have wrought." The breeze leapt past each of them in turn, ruffling Papa's beard, blowing up Mama's caftan so that she shrieked, tugging at the ends of Kak Ayu's scarf, tweaking Alia's nose so that she sneezed.

"Oh dear, oh dear, oh dear," the voice sighed. "When will you learn? If your door can't be closed to the darkness . . ."

There was a loud bang as the doors to the house were thrown wide open. "Then you might as well just let it in," the voice boomed.

There was a pause.

Then Mama screamed and pushed her chair back, the harsh scraping sound of wood against tile tearing through the night. "Abang! What in the world—"

Papa only grunted in response.

"What's the—" Alia's eyes finally caught up with her mouth, and she stared in horror. Because Papa was shoving food into his mouth by the handful, rice and curry and sambal and ulam. He didn't seem to mind that bits of glass glinted in the food; he just kept cramming it all in without chewing, more and more until his cheeks ballooned wildly, all with a completely nonchalant look on his face. It would have been funny, if it wasn't completely terrifying.

"Papa?" she whispered.

At the sound of her voice, Papa went completely still. The only sound in the room was that of his thick, ragged breathing, as if his chest was filled with spider-webs.

Then he snapped his neck around to look at Alia, and she shrank back in horror. Because Papa's eyes were completely blank—lights off, nobody's home—just like Charlene's before, just like Mama's. As if somebody had reached in and wiped them clean of any emotion. And as she stared, he smiled right at her, food dripping from his full mouth and dribbling down his chin.

"Ya Allah." Mama gulped. "What is happening?"

Papa swiveled his head to look at her, the smile still pasted on his face. "Papa isn't here right now," he said quietly. Bits of rice flew from his mouth onto the table as he spoke, and Mama recoiled involuntarily. She leapt up and beckoned to the girls.

"Quickly," she told them, her eyes never leaving Papa. "Behind me."

"Where are you going, sayang?" the thing that wore Papa's face asked. It spat whatever was left of the food in its mouth out onto the floor, where it landed with a sickening splat at their feet.

Alia's breath kept catching in her chest; she wished desperately that it would just stop smiling.

"What are you?" Mama asked, her jaw clenched.

The creature that was and also wasn't her father chuckled. "Does that matter? It's the same face, isn't it? You could learn to love me, sweetheart."

"You are not the man I married," Mama said, steely eyed and unwavering, and Alia had never been more impressed, or afraid. "Return him to us and go back to wherever it is you came from. You are not welcome here."

The creature threw back its head and laughed a laugh so loud, it echoed through the little room. Then in one smooth motion it leapt onto the table and began to dance a merry little joget, flapping Papa's sarong pelikat as it moved and casting weird shadows onto the walls. Plates and dishes went crashing to the floor as Papa's feet moved nimbly down the table, more nimbly than Alia had ever seen them move. She covered her ears, but it wasn't enough to block out the crash and tinkle of glass and porcelain, or the way the monster hummed as it moved closer and closer to them. *"Can't close a door against the darkness when there's something wedging it opennnnn . . ."* it bellowed like an opera singer, voice soaring up to the rafters.

"Can't stop the shadows from slipping through the tear in the veilllllll . . ."

"Mama," Alia whispered. "What do we . . ."

Then she stopped. Beside her, Mama swayed gently on her feet.

Alia swallowed hard. "Mama?"

Mama didn't speak. She just kept swaying and swaying, and the creature on the table laughed again. "Here she comes!" it boomed happily. "Here she comes!"

Mama began to hum.

On the table, the Papa-monster laughed and clapped its hands in delight. "My song!" it crowed. "She knows my song!"

And that's when the Mama-monster began to dance, her arms flailing with weird, jerky movements, like a puppet on strings controlled by hands nobody could see. The Papa-monster clapped its own hands happily to the beat. "Dance with me, girls," Mama sang, and her voice was a high-pitched whine that sent shivers crawling up and down Alia's back. Bits of broken glass and china crunched sickeningly under Mama's bare feet. Blood oozed from the fresh cuts. But Mama paid no attention to them, or the red footprints she left behind her. She just kept dancing.

This was so much worse than the night with the CDs; so much worse than all the terrifying things that had happened to Alia so far. Alia's horrified gaze met Kak Ayu's. "What did you do?" she asked, her voice trembling, as she backed slowly away from the table.

"I didn't do anything!"

"Then what's going on??" Alia's back hit the wall.

"I don't know! I told you!"

Alia's lips trembled as Mama came closer and closer. "What do you want from me?" she whimpered. Out of the corner of her eye, she saw Kak Ayu slowly creeping away. *She's leaving me*, Alia thought. *She's leaving me to die here.* And in that moment, she felt exactly how she'd felt back when she was six years old and realized her big sister wasn't coming back.

She felt completely and totally alone.

"Oh, nothing too terrible, sayang." Not-Mama stopped dancing and stared at her, her eyes blank, just the same as Papa's. "I just want you to *dance*."

Alia gulped. "No thank you, Mama," she said. "I . . . I don't want to."

"Didn't you hear what your mother said?" the monster-that-was-Papa hissed, and now its voice was deep and gravelly and above all, angry. It moved, closer and closer, until its face was an inch away from Alia's, so close that its warm breath misted on her cheeks. For a moment, she forgot how to breathe.

Not-Papa took one finger and laid it gently on Alia's cheek to catch one of the tears she hadn't even realized were streaming from her eyes. Carefully, oh so carefully, it brought the glistening drop to its mouth and licked it from its finger. "Can't close a door against the darkness," it whispered. "When there's something wedging it open. And now that you've let us out . . ." It grinned, displaying all Papa's crooked teeth. "Well. It's time to party."

And right then, right as not-Mama reared back to lunge at her like a snake, right that minute was when Alia ducked, sidestepped out of their reach, turned for the doorway, and ran as fast as she could.

Alia threw open the front door, her heart pounding. *I've got to get out of here*, she thought wildly. *I've got to hide, I've got to . . . to . . .*

At that moment her brain stuttered to a complete stop, and any thoughts she was having died, overcome entirely by only one thing.

Fear.

The streets were chaos. Friends and neighbors and familiar faces had all suddenly twisted into something unfamiliar. Auntie Beatrice from next door swung back and forth on her gate yodeling the ABCs, a dishcloth still draped over one shoulder and a wooden ladle clutched in one hand. Her husband Uncle Edmund pranced up and down the street neighing like a horse, still dressed in the sleeveless white top

163

and bright blue shorts he used to practice tai chi every evening. The auntie from down the street who sold nasi lemak wrapped in banana leaves on the corner in the mornings stood on a car yelling out a long and loving poem about bunions, and the uncle who delivered newspapers on his motorcycle at dawn danced passionately, cradling a cactus in his arms. He didn't seem to notice the way the thorns pricked his flesh. "My little baby," he crooned. "My precious one." They all wore the same blank eyes, the same wide, soulless smiles.

"What are they doing?" Alia asked aloud, the words catching in her throat so that she had to force them out.

Not-Mama's voice whispered suddenly in her ear, startling her and sending goose bumps down her neck: "It's not a party unless everyone's invited."

Tears prickled behind Alia's eyelids. "Please," she whispered. "I just want everything back the way it was. I just want my family back."

The monster pretending to be her mother smiled and stroked the back of her neck ever so gently. "Liar," she said. "You only want bits of your family back. Not the whole thing. But we like it here. We like these bodies. And we're not leaving, not quite yet. In fact, we want more of them. The whole town."

"We?"

"It'll be fun, sayang. I promise." From the shadows came others, more and more dead-eyed versions of people she thought she knew, hands outstretched as if to embrace her.

Alia yelped as a cold hand clamped tightly around her ankle.

"Alia." Charlene grinned at her from the ground, her limbs splayed out so she looked like a giant spider. "Come and *play*."

Alia whimpered; she couldn't help it. As the hands reached out to claim her, she squeezed her eyes shut. *Please*, she thought, *whatever is about to happen, please just let it be over quickly*.

And then she heard the *whoosh*.

Alia opened her eyes and muffled a scream. Kak Ayu hovered overhead. This was a bad choice of words; Kak Ayu's *head* hovered overhead, entrails dangling below. "GRAB ON!" she yelled, and before Alia could even think, she gritted her teeth, reached up, and got a good grip. And even though part of her was grossed out at the slippery, sticky feel of Kak Ayu's insides beneath her fingers, another part of her was relieved. *She came back for you. She didn't leave you, not this time.*

And then, before anyone could figure out what was going on, they were in the sky, leaving the monsters far behind them.

Kak Ayu's body was waiting for them at the play-ground when they arrived, sitting casually headless and cross-legged as if it were at a tea party. When Alia let go, she wiped her hands as hard as she could on her pants and tried her best not to think about what she'd been holding on to. There was a thick, wet squelching sound as Kak Ayu's head reattached itself to the rest of her.

Then a silence that was interrupted only by Kak Ayu's panting. "You're heavier than I thought."

"Sorry." Alia looked around at the familiar shapes of the playground's cubbies and swings and cargo nets and frowned. "Why here?"

Kak Ayu shrugged. "My first instinct was to go where we always felt safe."

Alia nodded. In that context, she supposed it

made sense. "It's just that this place isn't exactly . . . secure."

They were in the enclosed cubby at the top of the twisty slide Alia had loved best when she was little. On one side were rows of spinning Xs and Os on which you were supposed to play games of tic-tac-toe; Kak Ayu peeked between these now, surveying the silent streets.

"Do you see anything?"

"No." Kak Ayu bit her lip. "Not yet. But they'll be here."

Alia's heart felt like it was somewhere in her shoes. "You really think so? Then shouldn't we run away?"

"You saw how many of them there were. I don't think we can outrun them. Or outfly them." Kak Ayu bit her lip. "I don't know what to do . . ."

"What are they anyway?"

Her sister shrugged. "Jinn, hantu, jembalang, ghosts, spirits. Whatever you want to call them. Their world and ours share a border. Usually, they leave humans alone. *Usually.* But sometimes, the border gets thin and they cross over, and that's when they start making trouble. Slipping in and out of people's bodies, taking control and causing chaos."

"But why?"

Kak Ayu sighed. "I have no idea. But we have to figure out how to get rid of them."

"Can't you do it?" Alia gestured vaguely at her sister. "Since you're a . . . you know."

There was a silence. "I try not to use . . . whatever powers I have," Kak Ayu explained, clearing her throat. "The more you use them . . . the harder it is not to want to keep using them. And the harder it is to forget the hunger. And once you let the hunger consume you . . . there's no more control." She gripped her hands into tight fists. "And I need to stay in control. Always."

They sat there together for a while, shoulder to shoulder, their eyes glued on the street below.

"I thought you left me," Alia whispered.

"I would never," Kak Ayu said firmly. "Never. I just needed to get away and put my body somewhere they couldn't get to. I flew back as fast as I could."

Alia nodded. She was grateful; she really was. It's just that she couldn't quite stop thinking about the feeling she'd had when she saw Kak Ayu sneaking out of the house just now. How it reminded her of being abandoned by her sister all those years ago. How hurt she had been. And how, for just a moment, she thought she had once more put her trust in the wrong person.

They fell silent again, though their eyes never stopped darting all around, searching for enemies in the shadows.

"So you thought . . . you thought I was a murderer," Kak Ayu said.

Alia's insides performed an Olympic-worthy series of somersaults. "Yes," she said.

"And instead of asking me or believing me, you just went ahead and tried to get Mama and Papa to get rid of me." She was being strangely matter-of-fact about it, all things considered.

"Uh-huh."

"And you thought I was on their side. Those hantus."

Alia cleared her throat. "I mean. Technically, you are. You're a . . . a . . . well . . ."

"A monster."

"Well. I. Um . . ." This was torture. Alia had never felt so small and so miserable and so utterly *wrong* in her life. "I just wanted my life to get back to normal," she said. "And you were making everything so absolutely not normal, and spying on me. And you were helping me, but you were also hurting other people to do it. And then the voices started and at first I thought

170

they *were* you, and then I thought they were *because* of you. And if you went away . . ." Her voice trailed away helplessly.

Ayu nodded. "Okay," she said softly. "Okay." Her head snapped up to meet Alia in the eye. "I'll admit it," she said, "I'm not a murderer, and it's not like I summoned the hantus to start tormenting you. I really just wanted to come home and be part of a family again. But you were making everything so hard, and you kept rejecting me, over and over again, when all I wanted to do was be your friend." She looked down and fiddled with her shoelaces. "In my head, everything going wrong was because of you, and if you just accepted me, then life would have been perfect. And I was so mad at you. But I never wanted you to be scared of me."

Alia hesitated. "But you were spying on us, right?" she asked. "That's why that whooshing sound was so familiar. You've been watching me."

There was a pause. Then Kak Ayu nodded.

"And you did hurt other people, just because you were trying to help me?"

Kak Ayu sighed. "I shouldn't have done that stuff to your teachers, or to Su Ann. And I shouldn't have scared the other girls. I guess I just got caught up in making you see that your life could be . . . better . . . with me in it."

Alia crossed her arms. "And scribbling on Papa's photo? Messing up Mama's office?"

"Oh." Kak Ayu smiled, just a little. "Those, I just did because you were being annoying."

She leaned back. In the moonlight, and with the absence of the usual scarf around her neck, Alia could clearly see the thin, jagged line that separated Kak Ayu's head from the rest of her. "I could have just been up-front about everything from the beginning," her sister said. "Only for some of us, the past is a place we can't bear living in for too long, and even visiting hurts." She fiddled with the hem of her sleeve. "I just wanted to make sure you'd like me. Help you see what a good big sister I could be, you know? You weren't really opening up and I wanted to *know* you as much as I possibly could. I'd already missed so much. . . ."

"Spying isn't the way to do that. It's not . . ." Alia searched for the right word and settled for "Nice. It isn't nice. And doing stuff to get Mama and Papa mad at me . . . that wasn't nice either."

"I know. I'm sorry." Kak Ayu folded her hands calmly in her lap. "When I left," she began, then paused as if to gather her thoughts. Alia waited. She felt like she needed to hold her breath, that if she let even one sound escape, she would never hear the end of this story.

"When I left," Ayu continued, "I was only sixteen. A kid. I didn't know where I was going or what I was looking for. I just knew I wanted to get away. Mama and Papa had so much power over me, and I couldn't stand it. I wanted to make my own decisions. I wanted my own power." She sighed. "I was so angry, with the kind of anger that eats away at your insides and leaves you empty. And when you're empty, it's easy for things to come rushing in to fill the space."

"What kinds of things?" Alia whispered.

"Bad things." Ayu kept lacing her fingers together, then pulling them apart, together, then apart, over and over and over again. "Things I would never want my little sister to even dream of. And I fell in with people who told me how I could achieve those things. Get all the power I ever wanted. Never be afraid of anything ever again." She sighed. "The first time I flew . . . it felt good. It felt like I could touch the stars, like I could race the wind. It felt like the power I craved. But with the freedom came the hunger." Her face darkened then, and she stopped talking for a long time, so long that Alia wondered whether she was going to continue at all.

"You don't have to go on," she said quietly. "You can stop now. You don't owe me anything."

Ayu swallowed hard. "Yes, I do. No more secrets. They'll only ruin us all." She sat a little straighter and went on, eyes focused on a point somewhere on the wall ahead. "The hunger was intense. It was consuming. It wanted something very specific, you see, and I knew what that was, and I didn't want to give in. I was afraid of what would happen to me if I caved, even just once. I was worried that I'd lose myself completely, that I'd just be this . . . this . . . monster. Forever." She gripped the arms of the chair she was sitting on so hard that Alia wondered for a second if she'd break them right off.

"How did you stop yourself?" Alia asked, curious in spite of herself.

Ayu shut her eyes. "I thought of you," she said quietly. "You, and Mama, and Papa. I thought about what it would take to be able to come back home. I thought about how much I wanted to be back where I belonged. And I stayed away until I had it under control, until I learned to ignore the voice inside that told me to do the bad things, that wanted to be fed with flesh and blood. Until it got so little that I could pretend it wasn't even there." She smiled a small, tired smile. "It took a long time."

For the first time in ages, Alia felt like hugging her sister. "Is the voice gone?" she asked.

Ayu took in a deep, shaky breath. "No," she said simply. "Never."

They fell quiet then, and though she felt bad about it, Alia knew she had to ask the question that was plaguing her. "What about the things?" she asked.

Ayu frowned. "What things?"

"The things I found in that drawstring bag . . ."

"I knew it!" Ayu gazed at her accusingly. "I knew you were snooping through my stuff!"

"I thought you were stealing kids!" Alia sputtered. "I thought . . . I wanted to . . . I just needed you not to be a killer, okay?"

"Fair enough." Ayu smiled faintly. "When I do those night flights, I spend my time looking for people who may be lost and in pain. People like me. I try and watch over them, make sure they get somewhere safe." Her face grew sad. "Sometimes I have to scare them, so I can get them away from bad places, or from people who might want to hurt them. And when they run, sometimes they leave things behind. So I bring them home. Like little mementos. Reminders that even the most hideous creatures can do good. Even if . . ." She paused to sigh again. "Even if you have to become a monster to do it."

"I'm sorry," Alia whispered, her voice thick with tears. "I'm really, really sorry."

"It's not your fault. It's mine." Ayu shrugged. "I made those choices, and now I have to live with them."

"But at least," Alia offered with a small smile, "at least now . . . you don't have to live with them alone?"

She was rewarded with her sister's warm, wide smile, the one she remembered from the old days. She hadn't seen that smile in a long time.

"I guess that's true," Kak Ayu whispered.

Alia scratched at a mosquito bite, suddenly embarrassed. Somewhere in the distance, a dog began to bark, and the sound echoed down the quiet street.

Until it abruptly stopped.

Alia and Kak Ayu exchanged frightened glances and turned to look down below . . .

. . . where Mama and Papa stood. Neither said a word or made a single sound. They just stood. And watched. And smiled.

Alia was sure she stopped breathing for a moment.

Papa grinned as he peered up at the play structure. "Come out, come out, wherever you are!" he sang.

Alia turned to her sister. "What do we do now?"

Before she could answer, the creatures below began to move. They didn't shuffle like zombies in movies, but they advanced slowly. Alia had already seen first-hand how fast they could run. So why, she wondered, weren't they moving quicker?

And then it dawned on her: because they didn't want to. Because this was part of their fun.

"It's a game to them," she said to Kak Ayu.

"What?"

"It's a game. This is all just . . . entertainment. They're not doing it because they want to eat us, or spread a virus, or whatever. They're just doing it because . . . because . . ."

"Because a door was wedged open," Mama cooed from somewhere right below their feet, making them jump. "Because there was a tear in the veil. Because someone ripped a rift between worlds, and we slipped through, and found that we like it here." Through the gaps in the floor, Alia watched as the thing that was supposed to be her mother stared at her own hands, flexing her fingers as if testing how the skin fit over them. "These strange, unwieldy bodies! These silly, complicated minds! These messy human emotions!" Mama laughed delightedly. "So many fun little things to manipulate. So much chaos we can cause." Mama's neck suddenly snapped straight back, and she smiled a wicked smile directly at Alia. "We're never going to leave," she whispered.

"We'll take over the whole town," another voice said gleefully, and Alia shrank back in horror as she realized it belonged to Charlene, who had shimmied to the top of the swing set and sat on her haunches, her curls forming a wild halo around her head. "And then you and I can play, bestie. Always."

"Our own personal playground," Papa said, spreading his arms out wide as if he wanted to embrace the whole town. "Filled with our own personal toys. What riches. Why, our friends are busy collecting their own playthings right now! Do you hear them?" He cocked his head toward the screams and yells and raucous singing echoing all over town, closing his eyes as if he was savoring the finest music. "It's beauuuuutiful."

"Brings a tear to my eye." Charlene nodded solemnly.

"You can't do this," Alia yelled.

"Oh yeah?" Papa's teeth gleamed in the glow of the streetlights. "Watch us. We're going to have such a good time with this town. Only we want you to join us, sayang," he said in his most persuasive voice.

"We're a family, aren't we?" Mama purred, circling slowly beneath them like a shark about to sink its teeth into its prey. "Families should stick together."

"You're not our family," Alia said, stomping her foot. "Give us our parents back."

Mama laughed, and it was like nails on a chalkboard. "Well, if that's what you want." She smiled up at them. "Then I'm all yours, baby." With a single leap, Mama was on the roof of the play structure, and the whole thing shuddered with her weight. For a moment, nothing happened. Then suddenly Mama's hand burst through the solid plastic roof, flailing wildly between them. Alia and Kak Ayu both screamed as Mama cackled. "Hello, girls!" she trilled. "It's a reunion!"

Kak Ayu grabbed Alia's hand. "Come on!" she said, gesturing behind her, where a cargo net stretched out to another cubby. "We've got to get out of here."

Alia followed, trying her best to dodge Mama's arm, which still reached through the roof clutching at the air between them. And even as she stepped out to grab hold of the ropes closest to her, she felt fingers thread themselves through her hair and pull, hard.

Alia shrieked as she fell backward.

"Alia!" Kak Ayu came stumbling back toward her. "Come on, we've got to go!"

"I can't!" Alia tried her best to move. "My foot's stuck!"

She heard the sound of Kak Ayu sucking in her breath. "I'll help you," Kak Ayu said, bending low to try and untangle Alia's foot from the ropes.

"Thanks." Alia tried to control her breathing as her sister worked.

"Mama," Kak Ayu said without looking up, focusing intently on her task. "Is she following us?"

Alia glanced over at the roof of the cubby they'd been in before. "I think she's stuck too," she said as she watched Mama struggle and let out a stream of curse words she would most definitely never have said in Alia's presence otherwise.

"Good."

The rope bridge rocked and swayed. "You might want to hurry, though."

Kak Ayu grunted. "I am doing my best, Alia."

"I'm just saying, a little bit better than that may be necessary." Alia gulped. "We have company."

Along the outside of the rope bridge, Charlene was making her way toward them slowly. The smile never left her face. "Playtime," she whispered. "Playtime for Charlene and Alia."

"Hurry UP," Alia hissed at Kak Ayu.

With one massive tug, Alia's foot finally came free. At the same time, there was a triumphant screech from Mama as she finally managed to pull her arm out from the wreckage of the roof. She grinned at them, batik caftan flapping in the breeze. "Who's ready for some mommy-daughter bonding time?"

"You take her," Kak Ayu told Alia, jerking her head toward Charlene. "I'll handle Mama."

Alia nodded. "Be careful." She turned toward Charlene, who was now perched daintily atop the ropes. Except for the fact that her palms and the soles of her feet were filthy, and that she was wearing My Little Pony pajamas, she looked just like she always did when she was waiting for Alia to come to recess.

She tilted her head and bared her teeth at Alia. "Hey, bestie. I've been waiting for you." She hummed and swung her feet so that the whole net began to sway, and Alia yelped, stumbling a little on her feet. Behind her, she heard a cry and a crash, and prayed fervently that Kak Ayu was okay. "Ready to play?"

Alia gulped. Charlene seemed strangely calm so far; the last thing she wanted to do was change that. "Depends," she answered, wiping away the sweat that dripped from her forehead. "What do you want to play?"

"Oh, I don't know," Charlene said airily. "How about a nice little game of tag?" She leaned close, so close that Alia could see the strange blank gleam in her eyes. Her voice deepened to a snarl. "I'm *It*."

"You know," Alia said thoughtfully. "I think I'd rather not." Then she threw herself into the opposite side of the net from where Charlene was perched, shoving against the ropes with all her might.

It was just enough force to send Charlene toppling backward onto the ground. Just before she landed, Alia thought she heard something that sounded a lot like air leaving a balloon. And in that split second, she watched something like recognition return to Charlene's eyes, then bewilderment, then shock and horror.

There was a sickening crack as the body hit the ground.

"Charlene!" Alia fell to her knees, trying her best to see through the net. "Are you okay? Are you . . . did I hurt you?"

There was a wheeze and a cough. Then a faint: "No worries!" Then, fainter still: "I told you to be careful with these creatures, didn't I." It wasn't a question.

There was no time for any more reunions. "Run!" Alia yelled down. "Run away, and try and find a good place to hide!"

"But what about you?" Charlene yelled back.

"Don't worry about us. Just get away from here!"

"I'll be back," Charlene promised. "I'll go get help and I'll be right back. Okay? Please, just . . . just be okay when I get back." And then there was nothing but the hurried sound of footsteps fading into the night as Charlene ran away.

Alia turned to find her sister and gasped. Kak Ayu was cowering on the floor as Mama loomed over her, arms outstretched, a gleeful smile on her face. "Useless daughter," not-Mama hissed as Kak Ayu sobbed. "You took and took from us, and then you left, like a mosquito grown nice and fat from all the blood you sucked from our veins. And then you went and turned yourself into *this*." Mama gestured at Ayu, her expression scornful. "Look what you've done. Dragged your rotting carcass home and opened the door to so many others . . ."

Alia frowned. "But you were happy the door was open," she said aloud. "You said . . ."

And then it dawned on her.

"Kak Long!" Alia screamed. "Don't listen! Fight back! That's not Mama and you know it. That thing is just trying to make you feel bad so you give up! Don't let it!"

"But she's right," she heard her sister say quietly.

"She's right, and she's not." Alia strode over to stand by her sister, as tall and straight as she could. She looked the Mama-creature in the eye. "My mama is in there somewhere," she said sternly, and her voice shook only a little. "She's in there, and she knows what it's like to be in pain. She knows." Was she imagining it, or did something flicker behind those blank eyes? "And because she knows, she would never, ever say things like this to someone she loves as much as us. Because that's her kind of love. Like a shield that protects you from everything." She took a step closer and the Mama-creature skittered backward, squirming as if there were ants crawling in her flesh. "Come out, Mama," she said quietly. "I know you hear me. You're stronger than the thing controlling you. Take your body back. Come back to us."

Mama was tearing at her skin now, yelling and cursing as she staggered here and there. If you closed your eyes, you could almost hear two distinct voices: there was the high-pitched whine of the thing hiding inside, and there was Mama's own, rich and warm. And if you asked her right then, Alia would have told you that she had never heard a more joyous, comforting sound than that of her mother's voice ripping through the spirit's mumblings and moans. "GET OUT OF HERE, YOU BODY-COLONIZING LIMP FART OF A SPIRIT, AND STAY OUT."

There was a growl, and then a hiss, like someone letting all the air out of a balloon. Then Mama's body sagged to the floor, as if whatever had been holding it up suddenly let go. From below came the sound of a soft thud, and Alia glanced down to see a deep green snake writhing on the ground.

"Is that . . . normal?" she asked Kak Long.

"I don't know. What happened with Charlene earlier?"

"It was too dark where she fell to see."

Behind them, Mama let out a groan. Alia and Ayu looked at each other.

"*You* check."

"No, *you*."

Alia bit her lip. "What if she's still a hantu?"

Ayu thought about this. "Maybe poke at her with that stick over there first."

"No sticks," Mama said immediately, struggling to sit up. "It's me. I promise."

Alia narrowed her eyes. "Prove it."

Mama sighed. "I've been reminding you to vacuum under your bed for the last five days, and you still haven't done it."

"It's her!" Alia ran to her mother, Ayu close behind her, and fell into the world's best hug, the kind of hug that made everything better. It was the best nagging she'd ever received in her life.

"I'm so sorry," Mama whispered as she clung to them, and Alia could hear the tears in her voice. "Those things I did . . . those things I *said* . . . I could hear myself saying them and I kept trying to stop but—"

"It doesn't matter," Kak Long said, shaking her head.

"We know that wasn't you," Alia added quickly, patting Mama's arm. "We know. But now we have to save everyone else in town, and I'm not sure how we're going to do that." She felt a sob stick in her throat and tried her best to swallow it. Alia hated not having a plan.

"Now, just what have you people done with my sweetheart?" The Papa-creature's voice was loud and grating, and it made Alia want to throw things. He bent down to pick up the snake slithering at his feet and kissed the top of its head. "There, there, my love. They'll get what's coming to them."

Ayu groaned. "Not him again."

"Me again, I'm afraid." He leapt from his spot on the ground to the cubby opposite them, the snake now coiled around his neck. Everything shuddered at the impact, and Ayu had to catch Mama before she lost her balance.

"I'm fine," Mama said, shaking her off irritably. "Let go. I'm fine."

The monster hummed softly as he walked across the top of the monkey bars toward them, step by purposeful step. "It's too late, you know," he said, as if they were just having a friendly little chitchat at the neighborhood kopitiam. "It's already started. You may pull some of your own out of our clutches, but there are so many of us. What can you do but surrender?"

"We're never doing *that*," Alia spat out, and the snake reared its head back and hissed at her.

"I knew you would be stubborn." The Papa-creature let out an exaggerated sigh. "Oh well. If you cannot be subdued, you'll just have to be . . . supper." Then he uncoiled the snake from his neck. "Darling!" His lips curved into a cruel grin as the snake hissed back. "Time to eat," he whispered.

And the snake launched itself toward them, jaws wide open, fangs bared.

25

"Run!" Mama screamed, and before Alia knew it, Kak Long was grabbing her arm and shoving her down the slide, spinning around so fast that they slammed onto the padded ground below in a heap of tangled legs and elbows.

But there was no time to ask if anyone was okay. The slide juddered and shook as the snake made its way down after them, and the Papa-creature's chuckles could be heard from above. "You're never going to get away!" he called out to them cheerily. "She's hungry!"

They ran down the street as fast as they could, Alia, Ayu, and Mama, hiding behind cars, ducking into dark alleyways between houses. Yet the snake was always there, nipping right at their heels, hissing gleefully the closer it got. Alia's lungs felt like they were burning; her legs felt like they might fall off any minute.

"I can't keep going like this," she gasped.

"We don't have a choice," Mama told her. "Hurry!" They turned right and slipped quickly through an open gate, Kak Long signaling for them to be as quiet as possible so the snake wouldn't find them.

They were in the garden of a large, modern bungalow, the kind that Abah shook his head at and said they'd never afford in a million years every time they drove past. On the grass, a child's plastic inflatable pool lay abandoned, filled with brightly colored foam balls instead of water. A mini basketball hoop was set up nearby; there were targets positioned at intervals on the wall and toy guns loaded with foam bullets littered the grass. On a table beneath the porch, food sat in tin trays—mini hot dogs and burgers, cupcakes and potato wedges.

A party of some kind, hastily abandoned.

Except for one person.

Su Ann sat at the head of the table, a lighter in her hand. In front of her was a birthday cake, with three candles stuck carefully in the blue frosting. Su Ann had a little brother, Alia remembered. *And I guess he likes inflatable pools as much as we did.* But Su Ann didn't seem to notice they were even there. As they watched, she pressed the button so that a small orange flame burst to life at the lighter's tip; she lit each candle carefully and blew them out. "Happy birthday to you!" she sang.

And then she did it all over again.

Mama walked slowly toward Su Ann and placed one hand gently on her shoulder. "Are you all right?" Alia heard her whisper. But Su Ann didn't answer. "Happy birthday to you!" she sang, and in the flickering candlelight, Alia thought she could see tears in her eyes.

Alia swallowed hard. "What do you think happened to her?" she whispered to Kak Long as the lighter clicked and the candles glowed, one by one.

Kak Long bit her lip. "They must have gotten to her too," she said softly.

"And you're next, little one," a voice hissed behind her, and Alia turned to see the snake rearing up so that it towered above her, a wicked gleam in its eyes. The Papa-creature didn't seem to be anywhere in sight.

Alia backed away quickly, her eyes never leaving the snake's, her heart racing as if it was about to burst. "You don't have to do this," she told the snake desperately. Her foot caught the edge of the pool and she fell backward, right into the pile of foam balls. *Unlucky Alia strikes again.*

"Oh, you're right. I don't." The snake's voice was light, amused. "But I want to." And then it lunged, as fast as lightning, ready to tear into Alia's flesh—

But not fast enough. Alia's hand grasped one of the foam balls, as large as tennis balls, and shoved it with all her might into the snake's mouth. Before it could stop itself, the snake's fangs had sunk deep into the ball's squishy surface, and it reared back, its jaws absolutely and undeniably stuck around an orb of hot pink.

"Mmmmph!" it mumbled, its eyes narrowed. "Mmmmmmph." But there was no way to make out what else it was saying, because there was a loud bang as a foam pellet hit the snake right between the eyes. Alia turned back, her jaw hanging open in shock, to see a little boy standing there with a toy gun in his hand and a determined expression.

"Who are you?" she managed to gasp out. "And what . . . are you even doing here?"

The boy dropped the gun and his face crumpled. "My birthday party," he wailed. "No snake! No snake at my birthday party!"

At the sound of his voice, Su Ann paused, hand outstretched, flame still flickering at the end of her lighter. By now the candles were puddles of wax, their wicks barely sticking out from their neon-pink lumps. "Kai?" she whispered. "Is that Kai?"

"Jiejie!" The little boy ran toward Su Ann and launched himself into her arms so that the lighter fell to the ground. "Jiejie, I scared! Got snake!"

"Kai." Slowly, that strange blankness faded from Su Ann's eyes, and her arms reached around to hug her brother back. She looked at Alia, her face bewildered. "What the heck is going on?"

"No time to explain," Alia said quickly. "Get inside. Keep Kai somewhere safe." Quickly, she hauled herself to her feet, almost tripping at least three times in the process.

Su Ann grabbed her brother and hurried toward the door. But before she headed inside, she paused, and turned to look at Alia.

"Thank you," she said simply.

Alia blinked. "You're welcome."

Then they were gone, the door closing behind them with a firm *click*.

The snake lay motionless on the grass, the ball still firmly lodged in its mouth. "What should we do?" Kak Long asked.

"We—" As they watched, the snake's eyes flew open and it began slithering straight for Kak Long . . .

Until Alia grabbed a toy gun from the grass beside her and backhanded the snake into the wall. It fell onto the ground, finally, limp and unmoving.

Alia let out a breath. She felt like she'd aged a million years. "So that's how you can defeat them."

Kak Long shook her head. "Yeah, but it still seems impossible. Like, how are we going to do this for every person in the whole town?"

"We can," Alia said, setting her jaw. She'd just defeated a monster. She wasn't about to give up now. "We can, if we just do it one at a time."

"You got Mama to come out because she's Mama and you're her daughter," her sister pointed out, arms crossed. "What makes you think we can do the same for a bunch of other people? Especially if they're strangers to us?"

Alia bit her lip. Kak Long had a point. "Not necessarily," she muttered, even though it was starting to feel hopeless. "I mean . . . there was Mama . . . and . . . Charlene . . ." She frowned. Charlene . . .

"Who is also your friend." Kak Long clicked her tongue impatiently. "I think we should run. Get away from here. Wait it out until those creatures get bored and leave."

"That could take forever!" Charlene. What was it

about Charlene? Alia closed her eyes and pictured it once more: Charlene, falling to the ground; Charlene, the light in her eyes changing midair . . .

"And we can't just leave your father," Mama said quietly, and Kak Long sighed.

"I know. I'm just scared."

"THAT'S IT." Alia turned to her family, grinning broadly.

"What's it?" Mama asked.

"They get scared. They can get hurt, in the bodies they inhabit, and they can die. So when things get too risky, they get out as quick as they can, before they can suffer any consequences. If we convince that thing inside Papa that the body it's using is in danger . . ."

Ayu's eyes lit up. "Then they'll get out of it, and we can save Papa . . ."

". . . and then we'll be a whole family again, and we can work on a plan for everyone else," Mama finished. "Nice work, sayang."

Clap. Clap. Clap.

The Papa-creature suddenly emerged from the shadows, his slow, deliberate claps sounding unnaturally loud in the deep, dark night. "Yeah, nice work, *sayang*," he sneered as he picked up the snake and caressed it lovingly. "Nice work, *abusing* my beloved. Nice work, making a mess of things. That's one thing about humans. They never *learn*."

"And what is it we're supposed to learn from all of this?" Alia said, her words sharp with anger. "What great lesson are you teaching us, oh *wise* one?"

"Well." Papa pondered this question, one hand leaning casually on a nearby tree trunk, the other still on the snake, which he'd draped around his shoulders. "Suppose I were to throw this body onto this nice, sharp bit of broken branch right here—" He patted it softly as he spoke. "And then I slip out of it just as it pierces deep into his oh-so-soft human flesh and he begins to bleed uncontrollably from the wound. And then we all sit and watch the life drain right out of him bit by bit. Like juicing a tomato." He shook Papa's head sadly. "That would teach you how very fragile these fleshsacks you walk around in are, wouldn't it? That would teach you to appreciate life more. And to maybe just let us have our way with you, so nobody gets hurt." His eyes twinkled as he stared at them. "Good lesson, eh?"

Mama had gone pale. "You're sick."

"And you're the cure, baby." Papa winked at her.

Beside Alia, there was a thick, wet squelching noise, and then a soft thud as Kak Long's body fell to the ground.

The penanggalan rose into the air, entrails waving in the breeze, oozing and dripping drops of deep red onto the grass below. Her hair floated around her like a halo, and her teeth were bared so that her face barely looked like the sister Alia knew.

"Kak Long," Alia whispered. "No."

"You will yield to me," the penanggalan growled, and it was the most terrifying sound Alia had ever heard.

Papa stared at the creature before him, his face stricken. As she advanced, he shuffled quickly backward. "I . . . now wait a minute . . ."

"There is no waiting," Kak Long boomed. "Only the penalty to be paid for your cruelty."

"I didn't . . . I wasn't . . ." The Papa-monster tripped over his own feet and fell hard on his butt. For a moment, his eyes wavered, and Alia thought she saw a spark in them that she recognized. Just a moment. But it was enough to allow her to hope.

Until Papa threw his head back and laughed, long and loud. "Oh, you fools," he gasped. "You silly, silly fools. You think this is enough? You may have ousted a couple of us but you'll see. We'll always come back. After all, you can't close a door—"

". . . when there's something wedging it open," Alia barked, suddenly angry. "I know. We get it. You've

197

sung this song to us a hundred times by now, and I still don't know what it means. What door? What wedge? What—"

"Alia."

". . . who are you to use actual humans with lives and histories as *playthings* . . ."

"ALIA."

"WHAT?" Alia turned to glare at Kak Long. "What? What is it? I was on a roll."

"It's me." And Alia had never seen her sister look so deflated. "It's me he's talking about. I'm the wedge."

26

Alia blinked at her sister as she slowly reattached her head back to its body. "What are you talking about?"

"I'm right, aren't I?" Kak Long asked Papa, and he shrugged.

"Who's to say, really?" he mused. "What is right, anyway? What is wrong? Nothing but a bunch of strange human concepts that you get all tangled up in, when you're really missing the whole point."

Mama arched an eyebrow at him. "Which is . . . ?"

Papa grinned. "The pursuit of *fun*."

"And this is fun to you?"

"New toys are *always* more fun," he declared.

Kak Long tugged at Alia's sleeve. "All right. So the answer is clear."

"Not to me, it isn't," Alia hissed back. "Will you please tell me what's going on?"

Kak Long took a deep breath. "They always told us, in all the old stories," she said. "Remember? The spirit world exists side by side with ours, and sometimes they cross over and try to make mischief. But the reason they could enter so easily this time, stay so long, be so powerful, do so many of the things they've done to us . . . that's because of me."

Alia frowned. "How? It's not like you invited them in."

"No. But a penanggalan is born out of darkness. And it's the kind of darkness that's greedy. It calls to its own kind. It amplifies itself. It always wants more. I'm basically a beacon to these things. A wedge in the door, a tear in the veil . . ." She looked at the Papa-creature, who bared its fangs back at her. "I'm right, Alia, I know I am."

"She is!" Papa agreed merrily. "A door left ajar is so much easier to get through, always!"

"So what are you saying?" Alia knew tears were coming; she could feel it in the ache of her throat, in the stinging behind her eyelids. She knew in her heart what the answer would be, and she didn't want to hear it.

But she had to be sure.

"It means . . ." Kak Long lowered her head so they

were face-to-face, and Alia saw the same dark brown eyes, the same long, sparse lashes, the same tears mirrored in her own. "It means I have to leave," she said quietly.

"Again?"

Kak Long sighed. "Again."

"You can't!" Alia said desperately. She could feel the tears beginning to fall and she swiped at them roughly with the back of her hand. Alia hated to cry. "You can't go! You already left me once, Kak Long. You can't do it again, do you hear me? I won't let you!"

"I have to." Kak Long's lips trembled. "If I stay, we'll never be rid of them. Even if by some miracle we defeat them all tonight, every last one . . . they'll just keep coming back. The whole town won't be spared. You'll never be safe. And I need you all to be safe. I need you all to be okay, and for you to grow, and thrive, and do amazing things." Kak Long nuzzled her gently. "You can't do that with me around, Adik. I wish you could. But you can't."

Alia looked around for her mother. "You can't let her go, Mama, please." She was begging now. Her throat hurt, but it wasn't any worse than the pain inside her chest. "*Please*, Mama. Tell her."

Mama's eyes, always so watchful, so observant, had

grown soft and dim and so, so sad that Alia had to gulp back the tears forming a lump in her throat. "Listen. I am your mother. I would never turn you away, you hear me? Never. If you wanted me to fight a million demons, I would do it." She planted a fierce kiss on the top of Ayu's forehead. "But there are some decisions you need to make on your own. And if this is what you know in your heart to be the way, then I'm here for you. And I'll be here waiting, every day, until you can come back."

The Papa-creature by the tree chuckled softly, and Mama sighed. "And so will he. When he's back to being himself."

Kak Long nodded. She didn't say a word. Alia suspected it was because she couldn't.

"Well then." Mama did her best to blink back her tears and shook herself, as if to pull herself together. "If it must be done, then it must be done, kan?"

Alia couldn't say anything. She could only cry.

Kak Long knelt down then, smoothing away the hair that clung to Alia's damp cheeks. "Listen, Adik," she whispered, and Alia could hear the telltale quaver in her voice that meant she was crying too. "Listen. I read you a lot of fairy tales growing up, didn't I?"

"You did," Alia managed to sniff out. "You always did the best voices."

"I did." Kak Long smiled. "And all those stories had happily ever afters. But in real life, happily ever afters aren't quite the same. There's happiness to be found here, but sometimes you make mistakes so big that it takes longer to get there. It doesn't mean it'll never happen. It just means we may need to wait a little longer."

"But you'll disappear again." Alia shook her head, remembering the months and months of running for the phone every time it rang, hoping for it to be her sister's voice on the other end of the line. "You'll leave, and we'll never see you or hear from you." At that moment, she felt the unluckiest she'd ever felt in her whole life.

"That's not true." Kak Long held Alia's hand tight. "We're not the same now, you and I. We know each other better, don't we? We'll stay in touch, we'll talk all the time. You'll see. I promise." Her smile was heartbreakingly sad. "We'll do our best, until we can get our happily ever after too."

Papa rolled his eyes. "You humans have the cheesiest lines."

Mama coughed. "He'll miss you, really. Once he realizes."

"I know, Mama." Kak Long bent low to kiss their mother's hands. "I'm sorry," Alia heard her whisper, and felt her heart crack in two. "I'm so sorry I've disappointed you."

"Don't you ever say that." Mama held Kak Long's face in her two hands, forcing Kak Long to look her in the eyes. "Do you hear me? You've made mistakes, and you regret them, and you're trying to make up for them by doing what's right. That's all that matters. That you keep trying."

It took an age to disentangle themselves, because nobody really wanted to try. But at last, Kak Long stepped outside the gate, the first light of dawn just beginning to crack the night sky.

Alia stood by Mama's side, trying her hardest to be brave like her sister.

"Be well," Kak Long said to them. "I love you all."

And then she walked away, never once looking back, until she was nothing but a speck on the horizon.

And then she was nothing at all.

She was gone.

In the silence she left in her wake, something shifted; it was as if the air got lighter, somehow. Clearer. Easier to breathe, even with the weight of grief that clamped around Alia's chest.

Papa cleared his throat. "So." He paused awkwardly. "What did I miss?"

And for some reason, this made Alia laugh and laugh until the tears streamed down her face; until there was no laughter left; until she was sobbing as if her heart would break.

THREE MONTHS LATER

"I'm home!"

Alia peeled off her socks and, without waiting for an answer, bound up the stairs two at a time, almost but not quite tripping on the third-to-last step. She burst into her bedroom and grabbed her phone.

And grinned.

There it was. An email from Kak Long.

Alia flopped onto the bed, dirty school clothes and all—Mama would kill her for that later, but for now she was going to enjoy Kak Long's missive, from somewhere in the Philippines. Kak Long wrote about the people, and about the little ones she taught English to; she wrote about the food she was trying and the friends she was making, though she didn't intend to stay much longer. *It's best, I feel, to just keep moving,* the email said, *until my feet take me back home again. When it's safe.* Kak Long's emails always spoke of when and not if, always confident the day would come, so that Alia believed it wholeheartedly too.

As she typed her response, racking her brain to think about what Kak Long might enjoy reading, Alia thought about what her mama had said to her that day, after the dust had settled and all their neighbors had gone home, as they swept up the shattered, broken pieces of their house and their lives into so many black trash bags.

"How are we going to bear it?" Alia had asked her. The ache in her heart was so great that she thought it might never go away, and she wasn't sure how she was going to wake up the next day, and the next, and the next, knowing this was how she would be feeling every time.

Mama thought about this for a while. "Well," she said. "We do what we must, as her family. We do what we would do when any one of us makes mistakes, even the ones that seem like they're irreparable. We pray for our loved ones, and we hope for them, and we grieve for them, and we fight for them, and we love them anyway, through all of it."

And so that's what Alia was going to do, every day, until the day Kak Long could finally come home.

The email was done. All it needed was her sign-off.

"Alia! Cepat, lunch is ready!" her mother bellowed from downstairs. She heard the front door open with a thud and Papa's trademark footsteps, heavy and determined.

"Smells good," he said.

"Alia! Hurry up! Your father is home!"

"Coming!" Alia yelled back. She typed up one last thing, then hit send and threw the phone on her bed. "I'm coming!"

For just a moment, the final words lingered on the screen, until there was a quiet *whoosh* of an email being sent, and the phone went dark.

Love, your sister Alia.

EPILOGUE

Melur blinked. She felt bruised and broken, her throat dry, her heart still pounding. "How did you know?" she whispered.

"Know?" The Witch—for that was who she was—regarded her with one raised eyebrow. "Know about your brother, who ran away? About all the fights you've had with your mother? The guilt you feel when you cause her pain, the hurt when she focuses on him when he was the one who left? The resentment? The ache when you think about the fact that he may never come back? And through it all, the fear—" The Witch closed her eyes for just a moment, as if she was tasting the best thing in the world. "Oh all that delicious fear, that deep, rich fear that you are simply not enough, that you are not the child she really wanted to stay at all, that she would have been happier if you were gone?"

Melur couldn't speak. Tears stuck in her throat and choked her.

The Witch stood from her rocking chair and walked toward her with excruciatingly slow steps. The flames in the fireplace flared, and for a minute the shadow she cast against the wall of Cabin 23 looked like that of a floating head, one with tentacle-like shapes dangling from its neck. As Melur watched, the Witch still walked, but the shadow paused, turned toward her, and grinned.

Melur wanted to run, but for some reason she couldn't bring herself to move.

The Witch bent down so her face was inches away from Melur's, so close that Melur could feel the breath misting on her cheek, so close she could see the hunger in the Witch's eyes. "So much easier," she said softly, tracing a line with the point of one sharp nail against Melur's cheek. "So much easier when a child simply believes and gives in to their fear instead of denying the darkness what it demands. So much less work for me."

Melur couldn't help it. She whimpered.

"Time to eat," the Witch whispered.

Melur closed her eyes.

ABOUT THE AUTHOR

HANNA ALKAF is a writer from Malaysia, where *Tales from Cabin 23: Night of the Living Head* is set. She is also the author of the middle grade novels *Hamra and the Jungle of Memories* and *The Girl and the Ghost* and the young adult novels *The Weight of Our Sky* and *Queen of the Tiles*. Hanna lives in Kuala Lumpur with her family and can be visited at hannaalkaf.com.